Xea

in the Library of All Human Knowledge

The MAC Series -- Book 2

S F Chapman

striped
Cat
Press

www.stripedcatpress.com

Xea in the Library of All Human Knowledge
The MAC Series – Book 2
by
S F Chapman
is also available as a Kindle eBook

Learn more about the author at www.sfchapman.com

Cover by Mae Yamo

Striped Cat Press
First paperback edition, First Printing:
October 2015
P1e1pd

Works by S F Chapman

Literary fiction:
I'm here to help

The Missive in the Margins
(Coming soon)

Science fiction:
The Free City Series:
The Ripple in Space-Time

Torn From On High

The MAC Series:
Floyd 5.136

*Xea in the Library
of All Human Knowledge*

Beyond the Habitable Limit
(Coming in 2016)

Contemporary fiction:
On the Back of the Beast

To David,
a new and talented young engineer.

Acknowledgments

Writing a novel, especially one in the science fiction genre, is a weird and sometimes quite trying undertaking. *Xea in the Library of All Human Knowledge -- The MAC Series Book 2* was no exception.

Fortunately I had help.

One of my editors suggested after reading through the first book in the series that the story of the MAC clones should reveal itself like the layers of an onion. *Floyd 5.136 -- The MAC Series Book 1* is at the center of the onion with the characters confined to a small and well-defined space. By the end of that book they have moved outward to the next layer and discovered a larger domain with many more possibilities and perils.

As *Xea in the Library of All Human Knowledge* begins the ancient MAC clones are just beginning to explore the immense area beyond their well-known realm.

When I was at last satisfied with the results of many months of work at the keyboard I turned the manuscript over to my three editors. Mark, Clint and Christina each had their chance to make changes and adjustments.

Xea in the Library of All Human Knowledge is certainly much better because of their excellent work.

Thank you all.

Please note:

If, by chance, you have not yet read *Floyd 5.136,* which is the first book in the MAC Series, may I suggest that doing so will greatly increase your understanding of the characters in the series and nature of their unusual situation.

Thank you,

SF Chapman

Introduction

At last the truth had been revealed.

The little group had only just discovered that they had somehow survived the horrific end of humankind more than sixteen thousand years before.

Now the tall Australian doctor, the stoic engineer, the visual artist, the bumbling surfer, the affable secretary, the gregarious restaurateur, the elderly tinkerer and the reticent school teacher finally knew of the precariousness of their peculiar situation: they were some of the *very* few remaining members of the species.

More alarming still was the creeping realization that they were now solely responsible for the future of all of mankind.

It was frighteningly clear that the ancient protocols and dogmas of past generations had led to the destruction of virtually all humans. What was needed was a new and different point of view.

A petite dark-haired girl named Xea would provide much of this fresh perspective.

*Luck, it seems, is a needy creature:
never are we rewarded without
paying a high price for the bounty.*

1. Fortuity demands compensation

It had been an astonishing three days.

Floyd watched another ocean wave gradually rise into a tall and murky ridge before forward momentum and gravity caused it to cascade down upon the shimmering black sand beach as a crashing whitecap.

The undertow tugged the foamy liquid tumult backwards to begin the cycle again.

The hypnotic steadiness of the ever-moving sea provided a pleasant interlude to the weary twenty-nine-year-old engineer as he lounged on the canvas armchair in the open front of the little hut. He chuckled; as impressive as the tireless ocean and the Polynesian paradise that adjoined it seemed, they were both fake; built by the seven of them over thousands of years as virtually flawless proxies for the long lost originals on Earth.

An astounding and immensely exhausting three days, Floyd noted.

He and his beloved mate Marie had nearly been killed after they had ventured into the mysterious and airless new tunnel network clad in the rudimentary space suits that he had recently constructed.

While the others had listened to the star-crossed expedition using the crude radio set from the safety of the Rocky Mountain Camp Habitat, he and Marie had been set upon by several of the ordinarily indifferent Minion Robots that guarded the passageways. The robots captured them and stripped off their space suits in a strange, dark chamber.

Miraculously, the small room where they were held hostage had breathable air.

In an amusing twist of fate, the group's feline, an especially intelligent and genderless clone whom they referred to merely as 'Kat,' had somehow found its own way into the chamber just before them.

That's when Floyd and Marie had learned the truth about their cryptic world.

The dark chamber was the lair of the Master/Minion, a super computer-like entity that had secretly managed their world for eons. As a final act of control over Floyd and Marie, the Master/Minion directed the robots to sedate them and activate the long dormant biorobotic interfaces in their brains. When they awoke, both could communicate directly with the cyber overseer of their world.

Suddenly it all made sense.

For a hundred and forty-two centuries Floyd's tiny group of seven clones had toiled alone in their small and enigmatic world. They had been unaware that humanity had been obliterated long ago by the secret assassin's weapon gone amuck known as the z-pathogen. They had ceased to speculate about their unexplained situation thousands of years ago. The group members lived rather ordinary lives and, when old age or accidents interceded, died ordinary deaths.

Floyd and his companions always started out in a very unusual and unhuman-like way. A huge mound of soft gray filaments that they called 'the Cotton' would sporadically produce large silken cocoons that would yield perfect adult copies of the seven members. The clones would be endowed with all of the skills and memories of an adult as well.

Each new clone started out as a twenty-five-year-old: marked behind the right ear with a sort of model and serial number, although they all preferred to call them 'version' and 'sequence' numbers.

He was currently known as Floyd 5.136, the one hundred and thirty-sixth copy of the fifth version. The clones always possessed all of the accumulated memories of the previous version but none from the prior sequence. Hence he could clearly recall only five past lifetimes, not the nearly five hundred that all of the various Floyds had endured.

Everything had changed three years ago when the Cotton unexpectedly produced someone new called Marie 2.3. Floyd had quickly fallen in love with the tall and talented Australian doctor. The woman's startling arrival precipitated extraordinary events that had led to the discovery of the Master/Minion.

As he studied the tireless mock sea, Floyd brooded over the sudden demise of his species.

It had already been too late when the doomed humans of Earth and the space colonies discovered the deadly spread of the z-pathogen in 3065. Several lunar scientists hurriedly instructed the various robotic research space stations to cease all other operations and run only the 'Phaeton Project,' a hastily created effort to reproduce the only known humans who were immune to the fatal epidemic: the archaic and very rare Mildly Altered Clones from the mid twenty-first century who were often referred to simply as 'MACs.' To nurture and protect the few remaining members of the species, the Master/Minions were directed to allow the humans to develop small societies unaware of each other and the horrific end of humanity.

Floyd and Marie alone had discovered the long hidden lair of the Master/Minion on the Cerces 4 and learned of the dismal end of mankind.

He ruminated over the frightening implications of the unexpected discovery.

Now he and Marie were solely accountable for the future of the few remaining members of humanity.

• • •

"I guess Marie and I are in charge of the whole mess now," Floyd pensively noted as he stared at the tall black vertical cylinder that was the embodiment of the Master/Minion.

Sabina smirked, "Watch out everyone, we're in big trouble." The petite red-haired middle-aged artist played her hands slowly over the large dark object. "Now what, oh mighty engineer?"

"I don't really know," the lanky man shook his head. "We're just starting to figuring out how to use the brain interface to communicate with the Master/Minion." Floyd absentmindedly rubbed the back of his skull.

"I have to say," Sabina scowled, "I'm still quite disturbed by the idea that we were all cloned by the Cotton with that jumble of spaghetti in our heads to monitor and record every little hiccup and heartache." She tapped appraisingly on the smooth surface. "This thing has been clandestinely snooping about inside of my head for eons without first being invited in by the landlady."

She stared accusingly at Floyd.

"It wasn't really snooping," he slowly said, "I guess it was more like monitoring. We *were* considered to be test subjects after all."

"I don't like being treated like a lab animal either," she huffed indignantly.

"The unusual events that led to our unwitting participation in this endeavor may yet restore our species." Floyd noted.

She glared at the black cylinder, "I *never* agreed to any of this."

Floyd grinned at the feisty woman. Before Marie's arrival, he and Sabina had occasionally shared brief and fiery liaisons. But that had all changed when the doctor had won his heart shortly after her arrival. Now he thought of Sabina as more of a very spirited and talented sister rather than a past lover.

"Sabina; I hope that you will join the rest of the group in the Rocky Mountain Camp for a dinner meeting to discuss our situation."

She cringed at the invitation, "Will Jake and Mia be there?"

Floyd nodded. The raw emotional wound caused by the recent and spectacular failure of Jake and Sabina's relationship was painfully obvious.

She stared pleadingly at him for several seconds. "Now that we know that there is something more beyond the stifling confines of this little hellhole," she whispered, "I want you to get me out of here."

He sighed. She wasn't the only group member clamoring with demands. "I'll see what I can do. First off, Marie and I would like to have Nick reabsorbed by the Cotton. Since he's so old and worn out we think it should be done right away."

Her earlier burst of anger had subsided and the clever woman considered the prospect, "I'm guessing that if you two can command the Cotton to reabsorb Nick, you can also instruct the Master/Minion to modify him when he is cloned again."

"I hadn't thought of that."

Sabina enjoyed her shrewd deduction, "I suspect that he will want to father some children."

The man nodded, "Since Xea was born about three years ago as the first and only non-clone of the group, Nick has mentioned several times that he'd like to have a few tikes of his own."

"If you can pull off that little biological alteration," she observed, "I will bet you money that Mia will plead for the same privilege."

Floyd stroked his scruffy chin in thought, "Without a doubt, Mia will want to have kids."

• • •

"Well," Dr. Marie Mayfield smiled at the Ynez, "you're about two months pregnant."

The expectant mother slumped in dismay, "I'm not sure that I can handle a second child."

They could both hear the raucous sounds of Ynez's three-year-old daughter Xea as she clattered around on the flagstone patio of the tiny cottage with her father and Uncle Osman. The omnipresent Kat scrutinized the rowdy spectacle from the canvas armchair.

The doctor watched the two men through the open door as they played chase with the tiny girl. Xea looked like a nearly perfect miniature copy of her Japanese-American mother, Marie mused, but their personalities were glaringly different. The precocious and rambunctious toddler was nearly always an amusing tornado of noisy and insightful activity. Ynez was introspective and deferential; sometimes painfully so, Marie noted, often quietly enduring the unintended misdeeds of others in order to avoid drawing attention to her own unhappiness.

"You'll do fine," Marie kissed the forehead of the pensive woman. "The second is rarely like the first."

A tremendous screech of agony interrupted the two women. A moment later Old Floyd carried his sobbing daughter into the cool and subdued adobe.

Marie tilted her head towards the much older identical twin of her mate, "What happened?"

The gray and balding engineer held the writhing ragamuffin out for the doctor to examine, "She fell and scraped her knee."

"Xea," Marie calmly appraised the crying child, "would you like me to bandage your ouchy?"

The toddler stopped squalling and nodded feebly to her aunt.

Within ten minutes the three-year-old was gleefully pirouetting about on the patio, a wide stripe of gauze fastened securely around her knee.

• • •

"One of the biggest problems that will hinder further exploration," Floyd grimaced as he talked to his twin, Old Floyd, and the wheelchair bound ninety-three-year-old Nick, "is the loss of the two space suits."

Nick agreed, "Yeah; that was an especially bad bit of luck for you two when you stumbled upon the Master/Minion's chamber."

Old Floyd sighed, "That and the loss of the radio. It took me years to build it."

Sabina joined the threesome at the sturdy table behind the log cabin, "Where is everybody?"

"Old Mia, Ynez and Xea are in the house preparing the feast with Osman," Nick reported. "I haven't seen Jake or Mia yet."

They turned towards the cottage. Strangely, a Minion Robot hovered inconspicuously some distance away in the profusion of pine trees.

Nick pointed to the unexpected visitor to the habitat, "What's that all about?"

"I don't know." Floyd said. He pressed his fingertips to his forehead and inquired of the Master/Minion about the robot. "Apparently someone commanded our mechanical interloper to come here."

Marie hiked up the rocky trail to the table. She stopped and studied the robot before she joined the others at the table, "Good evening everyone. What's the mechanical snoop doing in the habitat?"

"We were just going to ask you the same question," Nick mused.

The woman shrugged, "I have no idea."

Osman and Ynez carried huge plates of food to the table just as Mia and Jake arrived. Old Mia shuffled slowly from the cabin firmly clasping Xea's tiny hand. The little girl broke free of the elderly woman and scampered to the flock of adoring adults.

Marie squatted down to welcome the energetic toddler, "How's your knee, sweet pea?"

Xea held her gauze wrapped knee out for all to see, "Good; but itchy."

Osman pointed with concern at the distant robot.

Floyd shook his head, "We don't know why it's here."

The little girl twisted her head around and grinned, "There's my robot!"

The engineer's eyebrows arched up, "Xea; you told the Minion to come here?"

The toddler nodded proudly at the accomplishment.

"How did you do that?" Marie asked.

Xea tapped knowingly on the side of her head.

Apparently the clever little one had figured out how to direct the robots using the biorobotic interface in her brain, Marie realized. The doctor had only recently discovered that the children of clones inherited a particularly well-developed ability to interact with the Master/Minion. "Can you make the robot go away?"

"OK," Xea glared furiously at the idle machine. The contraption spun around and hurried off.

"Very good!" the doctor complemented.

Osman and Old Mia had watched the impromptu demonstration of robotic manipulation in horror. Sabina smiled at the little girl's plucky commandeering of the machine. Jake seemed perplexed by the incident.

Old Floyd shook his head in dismay, "Why do I imagine that this particular talent is going to lead to problems in the future?"

The group eventually dined. When the feast was nearly complete, Floyd stood and smiled at the crowd, "Much has changed since we were last here just three days ago. First of all, Ynez has an announcement."

The demure woman stood and nervously fidgeted until the others were silent, "I found out earlier today that I'm pregnant again."

The others murmured at the happy prospect.

"Thank you Ynez, that's excellent news," Floyd remarked. "Secondly; it seems likely that Sabina will leave us at some point in the future to explore the great unknown."

The artist nodded to the others at the surprise announcement.

"Lastly;" Floyd continued, "due to his advanced age and failing health, Nick will be recloned shortly."

In her role as the guardian of the group members' health, Marie stood and continued for Floyd, "We discussed this with Nick recently. I have instructed the Master/Minion to command the Cotton to reabsorb our dear old friend sometime in the next few days."

The group quietly considered the impending loss of the old craftsman.

"But I just discovered an odd wrinkle in the plan this afternoon that applies to all of us," the woman continued. "Before being reabsorbed, he must decide if he'd like to be fertile when he is cloned again by the Cotton. If he chooses not to be, then things will remain as they are now; he will continue to be periodically recloned for the foreseeable future."

The old man stared questioningly at the doctor, "What if I choose to be a daddy?"

"After you hatch out of your cocoon, the Master/Minion will not allow the Cotton to produce any more Nick clones. This edict applies to all of the rest of us, as well."

Marie studied the eight others as they pondered the significant implications of the change to their future prospects.

Most of the others were deep in thought, but curiously Ynez seemed to be utterly horrified.

Marie caught Floyd's eye and surreptitiously pointed to Ynez. The man whispered something in the woman's ear and she nodded.

The stricken woman looked up at Marie, "Since we are now both fertile, does that mean that Old Floyd and I won't be recloned?"

The doctor gazed off for several seconds as she contacted the Master/Minion with the query. "Well; it seems that neither of you will be reabsorbed and no new clones of Ynez will be produced. But if our younger Floyd decides not to reproduce, he can be reabsorbed and recloned indefinitely."

"What is the rhyme and reason for that?" Osman wondered about the strange proclamation.

"I don't know," Marie said. "I struggled with this arbitrary mandate for hours but the M/M wouldn't yield any satisfying answers."

Floyd nodded in agreement, "It's sometimes maddeningly difficult to deal with our cyber overlord."

Marie looked quizzically at Nick, "So what will it be Mister Nickleby?"

The old man laughed at the keen attention of the others seated around the table, "I still want to be a daddy."

Mia waved her hand enthusiastically, "Can Jake and I be recloned as parents too?"

Marie considered the question carefully, "I suppose so."

Sabina burst into laughter at the exchange and pointed to Floyd, "See? I told you."

Jake seemed uneasy about the decision that Mia had made on his behalf.

They discussed the various plans that had been put forth well into the night. Finally Old Floyd gathered up his sleeping daughter and he and Ynez prepared for the long walk back to their home in the Southwest Desert Habitat.

"Tomorrow I plan to be reabsorbed," Nick proclaimed with a huge grin to his companions, "I will meet you all at the Cotton Room in the morning."

2. Reabsorption

Marie opened her eyes.

Where was she? In the nebulous state that sometimes follows a deep sleep, she struggled to comprehend her current situation.

It was very dark, she realized. That ruled out her street lit downtown apartment in Gold Coast City.

She could hear the faint baritone snoring of a man. Was it Boy X? No; Marie realized, she was reclined on a soft and spongy bed of some sort, not the thin blanket that she shared with the two other exiles in the caverns.

Waves? There were the distant thunder-like crashes of breakers upon a shore.

She puzzled together the clues: sleeping man, darkness, beach.

Black beach? Her wits were slowly returning. Black sand beach!

Marie smiled at the tiny mental victory. She was in the modest seaside hut with Floyd in the Hawaiian Beach Habitat. The woman grinned to herself as she added, somewhere in the huge Cerces 4 Research Spacecraft as it orbited around the sun between Venus and the Earth.

Why had she awakened?

She'd been nudged out of sleep by the tidbits of a dream about an excitable woman named Jessica and some sort of impending misdeed; and Jasper of all people, she realized with a shutter. Why would she dream about the long dead henchman of her dreaded nemesis, Kurt?

The unremitting waves rumbled outside.

Marie finally shrugged and snuggled next to Floyd in the dark and reassuring refuge of the idyllic paradise.

She'd had many odd and hazy dreams recently.

Marie kissed the shoulder of her slumbering mate. She hoped to get a few more hours of rest. Tomorrow promised to be an especially poignant day.

• • •

"Oh this *so* exciting," Mia admitted to Marie. "I guess it's also sad."

"Why sad?" Marie asked the elfin woman as they waited together for Nick to arrive in the tunnel just outside of the Cotton Room.

Mia stared up at the svelte doctor, "I keep forgetting that you've never been through our Reabsorption Ritual." She brushed aside some stray chestnut hairs that hung over her blue eyes, "It's sad because it's just like Nick will die. He'll be gone for months or even years and when he finally returns, he won't be the same old guy anymore. He'll be a young man with all of Nick's memories."

Marie studied the woman who's main undertaking for many

thousands of years had been to tend to the strange biorobotic life form that had produced numerous copies of the same seven people. The doctor nodded, "I've only been reabsorbed once. Floyd thinks that the Cotton may have only ever produced three copies of me. Twice in Kurt's Tribe and once here."

Mia smiled impishly to her tall friend, "I just looked this up in my records: Floyd's been cloned four-hundred and forty-five times!"

"Really?" Marie thought for a moment, "What about you?"

"There's almost always been two or three Mias around at the same time," she admitted, "but I usually live longer than Floyd."

"So how many?"

"Six-hundred and eighty-seven."

Marie shook her head, "That is amazing. You've been reabsorbed nine times, right?

"Yep. That's why I'm Mia 10.8, the eighth copy of the tenth version."

"So;" the doctor pensively considered, "you've lived through ten lifetimes."

"That I remember," Mia added.

"And more than six hundred that you don't."

The short woman smiled, "That's why it's a huge honor to

be reabsorbed by the Cotton. All of the future copies of that clone will start out with whatever memories that the lucky person had when they are reabsorbed."

"Does the Cotton only reabsorb old folks?" Marie wondered.

"No; age doesn't seem to matter, just important achievements."

"I guess you and Jake will be next," Marie motioned towards the Cotton Room door. "How are you two lovebirds doing?"

Mia lit up with a silly smitten grin at the doctor's question, "I've known the four men of the group for thousands of years, I'm not sure why it took so long for Jake and I to finally get together."

Several others joined them in the tunnel in anticipation of the arrival of the guest of honor.

Marie stared quizzically at the young woman, "You and Jake definitely want to return as parents and give up the privilege of being recloned again, right?"

Mia nodded somberly, "We talked about it for most of the night."

"Alright then; Floyd and I will instruct the Master/Minion of your wishes when the time comes."

Some distance down the shadowy passageway, Floyd glanced at Marie and Mia who were apparently engaged in some sort of weighty conversation.

Old Floyd reiterated the recently discussed plan to the younger man, "So it's agreed, I will attempt to somehow communicate with any other humans that may still be around beyond the boundaries of our spacecraft. Especially any possible survivors on the Earth or the Moon."

"Right;" Floyd said to the older man, "Marie and I will investigate the other groups of people scattered around the Cerces and figure out how to integrate them into our future society." He laughed unexpectedly, "Marie's surprisingly trepidatious about meeting people from outside of our group."

"Well;" Old Floyd said in sympathy with tall and attractive young doctor waiting not far away with Mia, "she *is* the only one who has experience with anyone else aboard the Cerces. Her association with Kurt's Tribe was rather unpleasant."

"More than unpleasant," the younger man declared.

"Here he comes!" Mia squealed.

A cheer erupted in the tunnel as the slow cavalcade arrived.

Xea sprang through the long elastic vertical slit that made up the aperture door of the Cotton Room to investigate the lively commotion. The jubilant little girl paraded happily around the throng of adults with the ever-present gray cat following closely.

When he finally reached the portal, Osman twisted the wheelchair around that carried Nick and backed through the stretchy opening. The others followed.

Nick groaned as he stood up, "Thank you for coming to my wake."

Sabina grinned at the old man's irreverence.

"It's quite an honor to be reabsorbed," Nick smiled as he hunched over the mound of Cotton, "and I'm especially grateful that you all decided to see me off today."

The group murmured appreciatively.

"Osman reminded me yesterday that I'm nearly ninety-four years old." Nick continued. "I can't say that I like it much. I've always preferred to be a strong and virile young lad and I've never done well as an old geezer as both of my dear house mates will attest, I'm sure."

Old Mia and Osman exchanged a look of uneasiness at the comment.

"In the last half dozen years, I've had to largely give up my beloved preoccupation of toiling away in my workshop to fabricate projects large and small for all of you." He reached out and tugged Marie to his side, "If it wasn't for this fetching young doctor, I'd have died several times over from various misfortunes."

The willowy woman kissed his craggy cheek, "It was my pleasure."

"In a few moments, with a little help from one of you young people, I'll stretch out in the mound of Cotton and be reabsorbed." Nick set his hand on the wheelchair in which he had ridden from the far off Rocky Mountain

Camp, "When I return in many months, I won't need this beautiful but exasperating contraption that Sabina built for me after I busted my leg." He smiled at the little group for one last time, "Perhaps I'll get around to joining Marie as she surfs on those magnificent waves in the Beach Habitat."

The ancient man slowly shuffled towards the Cotton.

Xea broke free from her mother's hand and darted to the bent and tired old man.

The toddler wrapped her tiny arms around his leg and stared up in earnest, "Goodbye, Unkey Nick. I love you."

Old Floyd hoisted his tiny daughter up to eye level with the gray-haired gentleman. Nick lightly kissed the little girl. Osman took his old friend's hand and helped him to gradually lie down on the silken mound. A few tentative strands of Cotton wriggled over his slowly undulating chest. Nick's eyes grew cloudy and fluttered several times before closing.

In moments, his slumbering body was completely covered; entwined and entombed by thousands of slowly twisting filaments.

Old Mia achingly lowered herself to her knees in front of the mass and mournfully stroked the vague gray cocoon.

The others watched the melancholy spectacle in silence.

When she had paid her respects to the elderly man with whom she had spent so many years, the old woman struggled to stand.

Old Mia stared at Nick's cocoon with somber funeral-like finality, "It's never going to be the same."

• • •

Sabina pressed her hand to her chin as she thought, "Sorry, kiddies; I have no idea when I last visited your littoral love nest."

"After the sad departure of Nick this morning," Marie remarked to the spirited woman seated on the blanket, "it's great to have you stop by for a lovely little picnic on the black sand beach."

"This has much more to do with business than pleasure," Sabina cynically noted.

Floyd handed each of the women a bowl of multicolored morsels and a mug of water, "With the help of our mental link to the Master/Minion we've discovered some information about the people aboard the Cerces that might be of interest to you, Sabina."

The man prompted Marie to begin.

"Right now," the tall woman announced, "there are a hundred and forty-one different human clones on the ship, with multiple copies of the same clone, the total number of people aboard the Cerces right now is," Marie paused to access the current information, "a hundred and seventy three. That's about nine or ten people in each group."

Marie grinned, "OH; this is interesting, there are five unborn babies in the tally. Apparently the Master/Minion has allowed a few other groups to dabble in reproducing using the old-fangled method."

"Sex for reproduction, how very odd," Sabina smirked. "How does our cyber-overlord decide which groups get the dubious honor of producing ankle-biters of their own?"

The perceptive query caused Floyd and Marie to stare at each other in surprise.

"That's a good question," the man finally admitted.

Marie squinted her eyes, "Our ever-attentive caretaker uses something called...the Hyperion Index. It's evidentially a measurement system for quantifying Societal Evolution."

A half-smile darted across Sabina's face, "How do we stack up to the rest of the rabble?"

"Ah;" Marie contemplated, "we are rated at 712 out of a maximum of 1000. We're ranked second to the Test Subjects in area number nine, wherever that is; they've tallied up 754 points."

"Really?" Floyd stared at the doctor with interest, "Those people might make good neighbors." He thought about the other group's implied superiority, "Why are they rated higher than us?"

Marie laughed, "It's not a competition, the Hyperion Index measures a society's progress. Group 9 is particularly chummy and they've developed some more advanced technology."

"I'll have to study the data about those people for myself,"

Floyd huffed.

Sabina had tolerated the abstract discussion of arbitrary anthropology in silence. "Remind me of how many laboratories the Master/Minion maintains for us lowly test animals."

"On the Cerces," Marie told the woman, "there are twenty 'Human MAC Test Group areas' as the M/M calls them. We occupy area number 17."

"Human MAC Test Group areas seems a bit overstated," Sabina said. "Could we perhaps call the different sections Kingdoms or Realms?"

Floyd considered the suggestions, "I like Realms. Kingdoms sounds too quarrelsome and medieval."

"Realms it is," Marie mirthfully noted. "Did you know that two of the areas are currently not in use? Realm 3 had a failed group that was not perpetuated for some reason and Realm 16, which was occupied by my former group led by Kurt before everyone was killed off, is badly damaged and uninhabitable."

"As you are well aware," Floyd reminded the guest, "we discovered about a month ago that long ago there had been some sort of battle with the Minion Robots that wrecked Realm 3 and dispatched Kurt and the other tribal members."

Sabina smiled puckishly, "I'd like to take up residence in one of these secondhand homesteads, hopefully the undamaged one. Maybe I'll put together a stable filled with enthusiastic young stallions to eagerly attend to my desires."

"We're not going to create a carnal play land for you," Floyd sternly reminded the woman. "This endeavor is only the first of many steps that we must undertake to turn back the near extinction of our species."

"Alright," Sabina sighed, "I suppose I can do my part."

"If we go to the substantial effort of sending you off to a vacant Realm," the man instructed, "I'd like you to surreptitiously evaluate various other clones for possible inclusion in our new civilization."

The woman moaned mockingly, "Do I have to be nice to the icky ones too?"

Floyd's eyes narrowed at the flippant comment, "Sabina, this project is of dire importance. To prevent humanity from disappearing forever, we will need to include as many of the remaining people as possible, however loathsome they might be."

"Yeah, yeah, I get it," Sabina growled with irritation. "Who shall I audition to be included into your polite and perfect planned society?"

"I guess that I only know about the members of our own group," Floyd sheepishly admitted. "The only one around with *any* experience with those outside of our little circle is Marie."

The dark haired doctor scowled at the unexpected attention, "My purported expertise about Kurt's Tribe is sparse. Other than sporadic visits with the Jake clone whom we are already familiar with, I lived in exile with two psychologically damaged mutes and had *very* limited contact with the three other thugs that made up that gang."

"Well we don't have much choice," Floyd conceded. "Who would you suggest?"

Marie methodically considered the various members of her long dead and dysfunctional former group.

"Definitely not Kurt. He was a violent psychopath. Even though I lived with 'Boy X' for years, I can't say that I *ever* really knew him." Marie winced, "The poor guy was beaten and battered by Kurt long before I arrived and he was never able to speak after that horrible trauma."

She gazed off at the restless sea, "Flossey was a dimwit. Jasper was Kurt's right-hand man but I never interacted with him, mainly because Kurt had demanded that he hunt me down. I guess that we should produce a clone of 'Girl X,' she was the twitchy but likable mute middle-aged woman who hid out with 'Boy X' and me."

Sabina shook her head; "I'm not planning on colonizing the great unknown with another woman."

The doctor suddenly frowned. "That's really strange," Marie stared out at the restless gray breakers.

"What?" Floyd asked.

Marie's eyes narrowed, "Jessica. 'Girl X' *is* Jessica. They were the same clone. I just had a strange dream about her."
"So the lads of the long-lost land were Kurt, Jasper and broken Boy X?" Sabina asked the woman.

The doctor nodded pensively.

"I pick Jasper then," the redheaded woman flatly stated.

"Sabina;" Floyd grumbled, "from what we know of these people, I think that Boy X or one of the women would be a better choice."

Sabina smirked defiantly at the man.

"Floyd;" Marie interrupted the verbal tussle between the insistent artist and the reluctant engineer, "didn't you and Mia know someone named Bashiir?"

"Yeah; he was the third person to be produced by our Cotton," Floyd answered. "He had only lived with us for about a year when he was killed in a bad fall. For some strange reason, the Cotton never recloned him."

"Well;" Marie's face lit up, "I've found him. He's fifty-five years old and part of the overachieving group in Realm 9."

"That makes sense," Floyd nodded. "Bashiir was a postdoc Experimental Physicist at Stanford University. He was a really sharp guy, which would explain why that group is rated so highly. I wonder if there is some way to contact him?" Floyd thought for a moment, "He was killed off as a version 1 clone before he could be reabsorbed so of course he wouldn't remember me."

Sabina shook her head in annoyance at the distracted man, "Before you start planning the Tech Nerd University reunion, can we get back to setting me up in a different

Realm, preferably with a Jasper clone, so that I can get on with appraising newcomers for you?"

The man considered the surprisingly sensible request from the woman.

"Fair enough," Floyd nodded to Sabina. "I have no idea of how we'll do it, but I think that we will eventually get you to Realm 3 to begin this project."

3. Uncloaked

Things finally returned to normal after many months of frenetic activity by Floyd and the other members of Realm 17. The chance discovery of the Master/Minion and the long shrouded circumstances of their existence on the venerable research ship Cerces 4 had led to a flurry of activity and innovation. Both Floyd and Marie continued to struggle with the opportunities and responsibilities as the human masters of the immense research vessel. Mia reported to the group that a new Nick clone would soon be released from the cocoon securely dangling from the mound of Cotton. Sabina continued to plan for her eventual departure. Old Floyd had been stymied in his quest to locate and communicate with any remaining humans elsewhere in the Solar System. Three-year-old Xea had been stridently objecting to her mother's distraction due to the pregnancy. Mia and Jake were reabsorbed by the Cotton to be cloned again as parents in the coming months.

• • •

Floyd chuckled. It just didn't seem that it should be possible and yet, amazingly, it had worked. After an especially complicated several hours of interacting with the still frustratingly mysterious Master/Minion, he had discovered this remarkably simple trick: he could use any of the dozens of Minion Robots that maintained their Realm as communication devices. Admittedly, overly large floating communication devices, but still a tremendous improvement over their few ancient wall telephones and the recently rebuilt radio set.

From his position in the center of the vast Junction Room

in the center of their Realm, he'd tested the surprising new system with Old Floyd in the far off Southwest Desert Habitat. His older clone had been expecting the communication and had quickly responded when the robot appeared before him on the little patio of the desert adobe. Now he was determined to try a more challenging experiment.

Floyd placed his hands on either side of the hovering translucent robot and imagined the intended recipient. "Find Marie 2.3."

His mental image of the tall woman faded and was replaced by a depiction of a far-off Minion Robot repairing a damaged light panel in one of the tunnels. The machine set aside the routine maintenance work and dashed away. Two minutes later, the robot squeezed through the rubbery slit of the Hawaiian Beach Habitat door and floated past the coconut palms towards the black sand dunes and the pounding surf beyond.

As if through the Minion's own eyes, Floyd now saw the doctor astride the surfboard as she waited for an acceptable wave. The robot messenger seemed intent on crossing the broad beach and venturing into the buffeting breakers. Floyd faltered, had he ever seen a Minion robot successfully traverse water?

He decided not to risk possibly sinking the man-sized machine in the warm Polynesian sea. "Stop and wait for Marie 2.3."

The distant mechanical messenger complied.

The woman turned into a swiftly rising swell and paddled

furiously. Just as the wave crested, she stood and lithely rode the board toward the beach. Marie leapt off just as the surfboard stalled in the shallows. She cocked her head and frowned, apparently at the unprecedented appearance of a robot on the beach.

Floyd chortled. "Marie!" he called.

He could see the confused woman scan the dunes for the source of the sound.

"Floyd?"

"Marie! I'm using the robot to communicate with you!"

The doctor reached down into the water and retrieved the surfboard. She trudged up the sands to the contraption. "Is that really you?" She scrutinized the device suspiciously.

"Yes! I can see you. I'm in the Junction Room and I just figured this out," he mirthfully reported. "Nice surfing by the way."

"Thanks...I guess," the woman hesitantly replied.

• • •

Old Mia smiled at the handsome young man as he feasted on the snack that she had offered him after she had extracted him from the cocoon.

She had forgotten how good-looking Nick was as a muscular twenty-five-year-old man.

"What are your plans, dear?"

Nick 4.1+ yawned and flexed his taut arms, "I haven't decided yet. I think I'll prowl around for awhile."

"Osman and I would *love* to have you join us again in the Rocky Mountain Camp," the old woman mentioned hopefully.

"No," Nick curtly replied. "A strong new body requires a nimble young mistress."

"I was afraid of that," Old Mia sighed.

"Is Ynez still playing house with Old Floyd out in the desert?"

The woman nodded with some annoyance. She was not at all fond of helping her hard-won lover find a new girlfriend.

A lascivious grin appeared on the man's rugged face, "What about Mia 10.8?"

"Reabsorbed just after you." The gray-haired woman pointed to the cocoon suspended in the cottony mound on the far side of the room, "I expect her to emerge in a week or so."

"I suppose that I can wait a few days."

"Nick, she's with Jake now!" Old Mia railed. "You just leave that girl alone. She's finally found someone who really cares for her!"

His azure eyes flashed angrily at the matronly woman, "We shall see."

• • •

Marie warily eyed the Minion Robot that hovered in the middle of their hut in the Beach Habitat. "Floyd, do we really need that thing in here?" she asked.

"It's only going to be here for a few hours," he grinned confidently.

Marie rolled her eyes at the engineer's most recent project that further cluttered their tiny dwelling, "I certainly hope so." She retrieved her red medical satchel from the wall peg, "I'll be back in a few hours."

Floyd absently rubbed his chin as he considered the impending experiment; he'd already used Minion Robots to contact everyone in the group. He smiled as he recalled having a robot stalk the evasive gray cat as it vaulted across the towering Victorian rooftops in the Cityscape. The recently discovered technique was becoming just an amusing distraction. He hoped to try something much more challenging.

The engineer clasped the midsection of the idle machine, "Find Bashiir." Floyd had no idea what had become of the man who had briefly lived with Mia and him thousands of years earlier.

Floyd frowned; the Master/Minion didn't seem to comprehend what it was that he wanted. He rephrased his request, "Find the current Human Test Subject clone known as Bashiir." A shadowy image flickered in his mind before it sharpened into a still picture of an elderly olive-skinned man. Floyd nervously considered the daunting ramifications that this test might provoke for in his long-lost friend and any others with whom he dwelt.

A flickering image that he recognized as the real-time output from a far-off robot appeared in Floyd's head. Apparently his friend was asleep in a sparse, dark hut. Hopefully the appearance of a talking robot would not terrify the man.

"*Bashiir*," he whispered.

The dozing man fidgeted.

"Bashiir; wake up."

The man turned to the source of the sound and blinked several times. He studied the peculiar visitor to his bedchamber for several seconds before he tapped on the side of the machine to assert its authenticity.

"Can you hear me, Bashiir?"

"Yes," the man shyly answered.

"Don't be afraid of the robot, my name is Floyd. I'm using this machine to communicate with you from far away."

"Floyd?" the still groggy man tilted his head in disbelief. "Floyd and Mia?" He thought for a moment before slowly smiling at the gently bobbing contraption. "I've had so many dreams of Floyd and Mia over so many millennia that I was quite certain that you two were actually from my past."

"I'm quite real," Floyd assured him. "Long ago when the three of us were version 1 clones, we lived together. You were killed in a fall and Mia and I haven't seen you since then."

The old man nodded, "My people have been expecting something like this for centuries."

"Really?"

Bashiir lit a small lamp and the cozy dormitory room brightened. "I'm Bashiir 6.32 now."

"Where exactly are you, my friend?" Floyd asked.

"The Sovereignty? I always thought that it was the same place that I shared with you. When I hatched out of my cocoon, you and Mia were gone and there was a group of five other people that had developed a rudimentary society. It still seems like a strange dream to me."

Floyd vacillated about what he should share with the man, "Through some unusual means, I know something of your group's achievements."

Bashiir grinned, "We have recently developed our fifth generation of worker robots. They're still ridiculously crude compared to the Minion Robots, but we use them mainly for repetitive drudgery."

They had built their own robots? Floyd cringed; apparently this group *was* much more technically advanced. "Who leads your people?"

"A charming and wise woman named Mixion is our revered Sovereign."

Floyd considered his next query very carefully, "How is it that you have been expecting this encounter?"

"Ah!" Bashiir smiled proudly. "Long ago Mixion surmised that we were part of a vast experiment and we've been expecting the appearance of others for centuries." The man's expression darkened, "Are you the experimenter or a fellow test subject?"

"No," Floyd carefully evaded disclosing his full understanding of the surreptitious circumstances that had resulted in the regrettable near extinction of humanity. "We just recently discovered that the eight of us were unwitting participates in a cloning endeavor.

"Amazing!" the old man exclaimed, "Mixion is always right."

The two men conversed at length about their societies using the strange communications conduit of the Minion Robots.

When the discussion died down Floyd said, "I will certainly contact you again, my friend. Hopefully several of us will meet you and Mixion sometime in the future."

"Well;" Bashiir fumbled unexpectantly, "I'm not sure that Mixion will be alive to greet you."

"Is she ill?" Floyd inquired.

"No...it's not a problem right now, but she has died twice in the last twenty years during childbirth. It's been quite traumatic for the Sovereignty."

"I believe we can discern when Mixion becomes pregnant," Floyd said as he thought of Marie's newly discovered ability to visualize recently conceived embryos, "we may arrange a visit then."

"What good will it do to travel here when Mixion is expecting?" Bashiir asked.

"I will bring an especially good doctor with me."

• • •

"Welcome back, Mia 11.1+," Marie congratulated the young woman.

"Thanks," the new arrival smiled.

Old Mia, Marie and Mia sat together on the low bench in the Cotton Room just after the woman had emerged from her long confinement in the silky capsule.

"About a month after you were reabsorbed by the Cotton," the doctor reported, "Old Mia noticed that one of the three cocoons was inexplicably deteriorating." Marie studied the now quiescent gray mound across the room, "She asked me to find out what had gone wrong and whether it was you, Nick or Jake that had developed some sort of problem."

Mia followed the story with interest. To her dismay in the past, the Cotton occasionally produced a cocoon only to reabsorb it sometime later without yielding a new clone.

"It took several weeks of tinkering about," Marie admitted, "but eventually I realized that the Master/Minion had discovered a significant defect in the Jake 2.1 clone that the

Cotton had produced."

"There will be another Jake, right?" the young woman asked with concern.

"Yes," Marie nodded. "Evidently the Cotton must regenerate after producing two or three clones. So it may be several months before the process begins again."

Mia slumped in frustration. "So just Nick and I were recloned?"

"Yeah," the Old Mia told her younger twin. "He was asking about you just after he emerged."

"Nick did?" Mia seemed unexpectedly giddy.

Old Mia scowled, "We both know that Jake is really a much better match for you."

Marie frowned, "I don't quite understand this sudden melodrama."

The two Mias exchanged a look of sad resignation; over thousands of years, hundreds of different Mia clones had endured the pandering ways of many self-indulgent young Nicks.

"He was lusting after Mia before she had even been released from her cocoon" the older woman reported to the doctor.

"Really?" Marie exclaimed. "Nick made a flimsy attempt at flirting with me a few weeks ago when I was fashioning some new medical instruments in the Fabricator Room."

She shrugged, "I just brushed it off as a crude boyish joke."

"He can be quite serious about pursuing sexual partners," the old woman warned Marie.

The younger Mia nodded with an odd mixture of trepidation and elation.

• • •

Several weeks had drifted by since he'd had his startling robotic communication with Bashiir, Floyd realized as he waited for his traveling companion. He was still at a loss as to how they would eventually find Bashiir's 'Realm 9.'

Old Floyd switched on the light disc on the center of his headband and tightened the left strap of his backpack. "You're sure that we can make this excursion in one day? Ynez will be rather displeased if I'm not back by tonight to help out with Xea."

"It shouldn't be any problem," the younger man wavered as he reconsidered the possible difficulties of the coming endeavor. "We're just going to examine the barrier door that Jake discovered in that odd low gravity area."

The men stepped through the aperture door from the warm and well-lit warehouse that Sabina had long ago dubbed the 'Lumber Yard' and into the cool blackness of the craggy and unfamiliar caverns.

The old engineer shone his light slowly over the towering rocky rubble, "I'm always astonished by the ruggedness of this place."

Floyd examined the vast broken formations, "I'm amazed that, until Marie came along and pointed them out, we hadn't found the caverns on our own."

They gazed at the forbidding rocky vista in silence for several minutes before venturing off.

The nearly identical men quickly developed a rhythm as they squeezed through the chaotic labyrinth of stony passages.

"How's the family?" the younger man idly asked.

"Well," Old Floyd puffed as he twisted through a tight serrated passageway, "Xea is definitely going through one of those toddler phases right now. Since Ynez is having such a bad time with morning sickness, they have been battling about every tiny thing for weeks." He finally pulled himself free of a constricted shaft and achingly straightened up, "This little jaunt is a pleasant break from the ongoing mayhem at home."

Many hours later, the twin engineers stopped to test the local gravity. Floyd produced a small steadily ticking windup clock, a long folding measuring rod and a small round weight. He handed the clock to the older man and scaled a tall nearby formation. Floyd unfolded the rod and dangled it down towards his companion.

"Marie and I tested this many times from one of the cliffs in the Rocky Mountain Camp," he called down to Old Floyd. "It took exactly one second for the weight to fall from the height of this rod."

"So anything longer than one second would mean weaker gravity right here," Old Floyd answered.

"Right. Let's give it three tries."

The little weight dropped noticeable slower during the tests. Floyd quickly calculated that the gravity in this

remote section of the caverns was about 62% of normal.

"That must be why I have a extra spring in my step," Old Floyd mused, "I'm only 5/8 of my regular weight."

"According to Jake," the younger man observed, "the gravity is even weaker at the barrier door. Marie noticed it too when she was exiled to the caverns in Kurt's Realm."

"Let's see if we can find that door."

The gravity was indeed comically feeble when the adventurers eventually located the sealed portal. Before they finally discovered the massive gray door, the two engineers each enjoyed making gigantic leaps from frightening heights before slowly drift downward to gentle landings.

"Why do you think the gravity is so weak here?" Floyd wondered.

"Mmm; the Inverse Square Law, no doubt."

The younger man contemplated the strangely out of place door in front of them and the implications of inverse proportionality. "That must be it, the gravity is weak here because we're now so far away from the center of mass of the Cerces 4."

Old Floyd nodded.

"We're probably getting close to the surface of the ship," Floyd speculated. He rubbed his big hand across the smooth surface of the barrier, "I wonder if this door leads outside to space?"
"Let's see if we can get this thing open," Old Floyd said.

The twin adventurers spent nearly an hour searching in vain for an activation button similar to those that had allowed them to open the other barrier doors.

"I suspect that the ship designers and the Master/Minion intentionally made these doors nearly impossible to open to keep any wayward test subjects from inadvertently draining all of the spacecraft's air out into space," Floyd theorized.

The older man tilted his head in thought, "A door implies that it can be opened to something beyond. I think we're missing a really obvious method of opening this thing." He tapped appraisingly on the hard surface. "Can you ask the Master/Minion about this door?"

The younger man scowled at the suggestion, "I'll try, but I keep running into problems when I inquire about this particular door."

Old Floyd turned to his younger twin, "Like what?"

Floyd closed his eyes to review the message that hovered forbiddingly in his head, "It says, 'Full information pertaining to Outer Hatchway 17 is available to Tier One Access Level Only,' whatever that means. The Master/

Minion is often maddeningly secretive about some things."

"What the heck is Tier One Access Level?"

"I don't know," Floyd shrugged, "Marie and I discovered that we both have Tier Two Access, for all of the good that does right now."

"Marie...She said something to Ynez a few days ago about communicating with our cyber overlord," Old Floyd stroked his chin in thought, "something about visualizing exactly what you want to happen."

"What? Like walking through one of the barrier doors?"

"I suspect that you're over-thinking the problem. Maybe something simpler and more specific, like this particular door opening."

"I'll try that but I don't think that it will work." Floyd pressed his eyes closed and imagined the heavy barricade slowly rising.

After several seconds, the massive gray portal flashed a pattern of colored lights across the surface, beckoning them to imitate the sequence as they had done many times before to open similar doors.

The two men stared at each other in disbelief before Old Floyd tapped out the pattern of the flashing lights on the door. The huge panel rumbled obligingly upward and the explorers entered a small, dark room. The long unused ceiling panels flickered on to illuminate the chamber. Floyd peered though a small window on the center of a sealed door at the opposite end of the tiny room.

"There's a long tunnel on the other side of this door," Floyd directed the beam from his headlamp through the window. "Oh! The Master/Minion is showing me a diagram of a tunnel network called the Outer Causeway." He pressed his fingers to his brow. "It circles the ship at the equator near the surface." A giddy grin flashed across his face, "This airlock leads to the Outer Causeway." He turned to the older man in triumph, "This is how we could easily travel to other parts of the ship!"

"That's great! But this is an airlock, right?" Old Floyd inquired. "I suspect that there is an airless void just beyond this door."

The younger man's shoulders slumped, "I'll have to construct some new space suits for that type of work."

"I guess we could use the Outer Causeway to eventually get Sabina to Realm 3," Old Floyd speculated. "Maybe even meet Bashiir and whoever else is in the various other Realms of the ship."

"Well; that will have to wait for another day. I think that we should head back home soon. After all, duty awaits you, sir." As he gathered up his equipment, the younger man turned to his older twin, "You know that I've been having such good luck utilizing the robots for various minor tasks."

Old Floyd nodded, "The communication system is working out quite well."

"I was thinking that I should try to have the Minion Robots fabricate some new space suits." Floyd adjusted the glowing light disc on his headband before he leapt off of the craggy ledge in the diminished gravity.

"That sounds like a good idea." The older man gazed back at the massive gray door before he sprang away.

4. The grisly past revealed

"It's been such a rough day," Marie lamented as she trudged into the little beach shelter that she shared with Floyd.

"Dare I ask or are the details just too sordid?" The engineer looked up from the thick journal as the exhausted woman collapsed onto the sleeping mat with the dozing cat.

"It's quite tawdry, Mr. Bernal."

Floyd bookmarked the page about space suits and set aside the journal. "Anything that I should know about, my dear?"

"Technically it's a medical issue, so telling you would raise some ethical concerns." She paused to contemplate the ramifications of the troubling information. "But the possible problems that it might cause in our little group..," her voice trailed off. Marie sat up and reached out to pull Floyd down onto the mat with her. The exhausted woman stared into his brown eyes, "This is between you and I *only*."

Floyd nodded his acceptance of her admonishment.

"After checking on Ynez this morning, I stopped by the Cotton Room to visit with Mia." Marie gazed out of the open shelter to the starkly lit ocean waves of the late afternoon. "When I got there, Nick was just leaving. He said he was only there for a short visit, which I found out later wasn't true. Mia and I chatted for a little while after he left, but she seemed quite nervous to me."

"Then she asked me about contraceptives."

"What?" Floyd stared at her in surprise.

"Apparently Nick pressured her into having an affair while she's waiting for Jake to emerge."

"Mia's terribly unsophisticated when it comes to men," Floyd sighed. "But she does have a long history with previous Nick clones."

He shrugged, "They are adults."

The steady percussion of the waves was slowly diluting the woman's tension.

Marie shook her head, "I don't know what's gotten into Nick. He was such a sweet old guy before he was reabsorbed."

"You're only familiar with him as a senior citizen," Floyd noted. "When he's younger, he can be quite a womanizer. Old Floyd told me that Nick made a halfhearted attempt to woo Ynez a couple of weeks ago."

"Really?"

"Ynez made it very clear that she wasn't interested."

"I'm really worried about two things," the doctor declared. "Jake would be devastated by the betrayal of both Mia and Nick. And heaven forbid, what would happen if Mia gets pregnant?"

"Yes;" Floyd's eyes narrowed has he considered the

unsavory possibilities, "we'll both have to watch over this situation."

An hour later they dined together in the shelter. When the faux sun slowly descended below the horizon, Floyd led the woman into the jostling waves for a sunset swim. They made their way out beyond the hectic breakers to the slowly undulating sea.

Marie leaned back to float lazily about in the warm oscillating water.

Floyd paddled next to the woman. "I'm going to have one of the Minion Robots build me a pocket watch."

She tipped forward and faced him, "A what?"

He laughed at the absurdity of the endeavor; "One of the robots will soon fabricate an old-time pocket watch for me."

"Why?"

"Well; first I'd like to see if I really can command a Minion Robot to produce something that is especially complex," Floyd smiled with self-satisfaction. "So I thought that a windup watch with all of the tiny gears and bearings would be the perfect proof that the robots really can make things for us."

"I guess that would work."

Floyd leaned forward and kissed the tip of her nose, "I eventually want them to fabricate several new space suits so Old Floyd and I can explore the tunnels beyond the airlock out in the caverns."

The weary doctor nodded, "I suppose that I could have the robots put together some medical provisions. That way I won't have to spend so much of my time manufacturing my own equipment."

They swam leisurely about until the sunset finally faded into a starry night.

Floyd led the drowsy woman back to the shelter. After changing into nightclothes and brushing out her long dark hair, Marie drifted off on the sleeping mat and soon dreamed.

• • •

"He's coming!" Jessica trembled with barely concealed terror.

"OK; hide over there," Marie directed her old friend to the shadowy area of the tunnel.

In the distance the three of them could hear the huge sinister man lumbering towards them.

Marie unsheathed her slender dagger and held it up as a signal to Jasper, her carefully concealed mate. She could hear Jessica franticly panting with fear at the imminent confrontation with the recently returned hoodlum.

For nearly twenty years they'd been free of the despicable headman. Relative peace had prevailed in the Tribe. Now Kurt was back and Marie was determined to carry out this brutal power play. She stepped into the center of the dim tunnel.

"Ah; my little bird, I haven't seen you for a thousand years!" the lecherous man slowly advanced, his fat hands reached for her breasts.

"DON'T YOU DARE!" Marie flicked the tip of the dagger into the sweaty man's chest.

He stopped and sneered, "So we're playing this game rough." Kurt's monstrous mitt clamped around Marie's wrist. His licentious eyes narrowed, "I like it rough, my dear."

Marie glanced at the silent flitting movement behind the huge man. Kurt snatched the dagger from the woman's hand, severing the tip of her left thumb as the blade jerked away. Marie dodged sideways just as the heavy metal pipe crashed against the back of the brute's head.

Shock jolted across the big man's face as he slumped ponderously to the ground.

Still clutching the stout weapon that had brought down the thug, Jasper watched the unconscious man twitch spastically on the floor. He set the bloody pipe aside, "Remember; keep my name out of this," the shaggy henchman pried the dagger from Kurt's fist and handed it to Jessica, "especially if you two want my help again."

Later, after they'd securely hog-tied the hulking man and stitched together Marie's bloody thumb, Kurt awoke. Jessica slit open the man's trousers with the razor-edged dagger as a warning to the man.

Marie kicked the supine man's ribs. "If you EVER bother Jessica and me again," she seethed, "I will castrate you in a most horrifying way." She drew the dagger swiftly across Kurt's bare thighs to emphasis the threat.

They left him bound and bloody in the tunnel for Flossey to later release.

The nightmare jittered and jerked.

It was many years later; Marie's hair was now streaked with gray as she laughed at one of Jake's odd jokes.

With a funny little smirk, she turned towards a sound to her right.

A massive fist walloped her mouth just below the nose. The gruesome sound of her jaw cracking resonated through Marie's skull. The surprise impact of Kurt's beating sent her tumbling back.

"I never forget a misdeed, my dear," the beast growled. "That's for cutting me."

Jasper and Jake leapt upon the big man, stifling any further assault.

Blood gushed from Marie's mouth and nose. Several teeth had been dislodged by the sneak attack.

She rose dizzily to face the abusive headman, "If this happens again, I will make good on my threat." She jerked her knee up into his crotch and caused the brute to grimace.

The horrific dream dissolved into frightful noise and turbulent black smoke.

The battle had raged for nearly an hour. Jessica and Ben were already dead.

A half dozen of the enemy machines had been eliminated in Kurt's hastily instigated war with the Minion Robots. Jasper had insisted that Marie should act as a medic in the ill-conceived crusade.

"GO!" Kurt yelled to Jasper, "DO IT!"

Jasper dragged the heavy container of explosives across the murky tunnel and lit the fuse. A robot lurched towards him. The machine's arcing appendages quickly dispatched the screeching man.

The explosives tore through the tunnel wall, momentarily stunning Marie and propelling incandescent shrapnel in all directions. Jake wobbled unnaturally next to her before he crumbled to the floor.

Kurt staggered to the ragged rupture in the wall. The last remaining Minion Robot cornered the tribal leader. Flossey lunged forward, driving a long crude sword into the midsection of the machine. The mortally wounded robot turned haltingly towards the young woman before it jerked to a stop.

"WE'VE WON!" Kurt held up his burnt and bloody arms in victory.

Marie turned to Jake. Her longtime friend wheezed on the floor. His eyes were glassy; a burning chunk of shrapnel had pierced his chest. She cupped his ashen face with her trembling hands. Marie was sure that he wouldn't survive the ghastly injury.

"Come on, let's go!" Kurt called to the two surviving tribal members.

Marie shook her head and pointed to Jake sprawled on the ground.

Flossey joined the big man and together they pried open the heavy door that the explosion had revealed behind the badly damaged wall section. Kurt wiggled through the barely open barrier before it snapped shut trapping him inside.

Loud hissing pervaded the wreaked tunnel. A deafening siren sounded. Marie gasped. Something was happening to the air! She slumped down over Jake. She couldn't breathe!

SHE WAS DYING!

Marie awoke with a start.

The distant waves crashed reassuringly against the shore in the peaceful beach habitat. She was still panting. It was so real, so *terribly* real. Her eyes slowly adjusted to the dim moonlit hut.

Next to her on the soft sleeping mat, Kat and Floyd sat together sharing the same disquieted look of concern.

• • •

"It was so real," Marie sipped the water that Floyd had offered her after she had recounted the nightmare. "I don't think that it was just a dream."

The man's brow rippled with apprehension, "What do you

mean?"

"I think that it really happened." She bit her lip as she considered the ordeal. "I was thinking about Jessica and Kurt just before I fell asleep."

Marie stared at Floyd, "Not that long ago, you and I explored that horrible old airless tomb of Kurt's world. So many pieces of that puzzle fit together."

She held up her hand, "The missing tip of my left thumb. No front teeth. Jake's wounds. It all makes sense now."

Marie blinked back the stinging in her eyes, "I think that the Master/Minion finally put an end to the conflict by evacuating the air from the tunnel and suffocating the few remaining combatants."

"Those weren't your memories." Floyd shook his head; "You never personally experienced the Robot War and the various tussles with Kurt. That all happened long ago to a different Marie clone."

"I know," she emphatically nodded, "that's what really scares me about it." Marie set the cup aside, "Somehow I apparently just relived the experiences of someone else."

Floyd stoked his stubbly chin for a moment; "Maybe the Master/Minion leaked that other Marie's memories into your brain while you slept." His eyebrows arched up, "You *have* had other dreams about Jessica, right?"

"Yes," the exhausted woman nodded. "I *definitely* don't want to go though that battle again."

5. Comings and goings

The robot deposited the trinket into Floyd's hand before it dashed away to perform some other necessary function elsewhere in the Realm.

He held the shiny new pocket watch in his palm and carefully inspected it. It was still warm from nearly two days of continuous machining and assembly. The beautiful timepiece that the Minion Robot had obligingly made for him ticked resolutely.

Floyd gently twisted the knurled knob to fully wind the coiled spring that powered the intricate array of gears in the clockworks. The engineer pried open the elaborately engraved front cover of the device. Twelve ornate Roman numerals embellished the dial face. It was a particularly excellent rendition of an instrument that had been obsolete for nearly sixteen thousand years.

A similar watch would have cost him close to a year's salary as a Graduate Engineering student at the University of Arizona in 2060. He closed his palm around the precious object and cautiously deposited it in the pocket of his trousers.

With the undeniable proof that he could command the Minion Robots to fabricate complex objects safely ticking away in his pocket, Floyd resolved to begin work immediately on the new space suits that would allow a thorough exploration of the Outer Causeway.

• • •

"I love sleeping here in the Rain Forest Habitat," Osman mentioned.

Nick nodded in agreement to the stout forty-nine-year-old black man.

"Sometimes when I need a little break," Osman continued, "from the chaos of collecting food and keeping up the many habitats for everyone, I come here for a little vacation."

Nick smiled at his dear old friend, "I've been thinking about living here permanently."

Osman frowned at the unexpected revelation; "You don't want to come back to the cottage in the Rocky Mountain Camp with Old Mia and me?"

"Well;" the much younger man hedged, "it's not so much *that* as needing a secluded love nest."

The older man laughed, "Love nest for whom, pray tell?"

Nick grinned lustfully, "Mia and I have been rolling around on the bed sheets."

"What's wrong with you?" Osman frowned. "Can't you leave that poor girl unspoiled for Jake?"

"Apparently not," he leered.

The big man clasped his philandering friend's shoulders and shook him several times, "You HAVE got to stop this nonsense." He set his startled companion free. "Let Mia be and come back to the Rocky Mountain Camp."

After the terse reaction of his best friend to the sordid affair, Nick relented, "You're right, I'll put an end to it before Jake returns."

"The sooner the better," Osman growled.

• • •

The little group was chitchatting in the Cityscape.

"I can't believe that you're really going to leave us." Ynez wiped her misty eyes; "Hopefully you'll meet the baby when he's born in a couple of months."

"I'm sure I'll see the little tike before I leave." Although she'd never considered the weepy woman to be a close friend, Sabina feigned a heartbroken pout to satisfy the required social convention. The diminutive artist brushed back the cascade of unruly red hair to reveal her shrewd and faintly freckled face. "Well, it's been a long time coming," Sabina halfheartedly whimpered. "I'll be happier somewhere else, I suspect."

In the idyllic park-like common backyard of the dozen or so grand houses of the Cityscape, little Xea tugged on her father's leg, "Why are mommy and Auntie Sabina crying?"

Old Floyd smiled at his tiny daughter. "When Uncle Floyd finishes the new space suits, Aunt Sabina is going far far away to live in a different place."

Xea tilted her head, "Can we visit there?"

"No; it's too far away," Old Floyd told her. "But I'll teach you how to talk to Sabina with the Minion Robots."

The girl frowned, "Who will live here and take care of the dogs, Dada?"

"Mmm," the man thought, "I think that Osman will stop by to look after Nudge and Noodle, sweetheart."

"What about Kat?" Xea asked.

Sabina grinned as she tussled the girl's straight black hair, "Kat takes care of itself." She cocked her head in thought, "Maybe when you get a bit older, you can live in the Cityscape and tend to the animals."

The girl displayed the fingers of one hand, "Can I live here when I'm four, Auntie Sabina?"

Ynez grimaced at her daughter's suggestion.

"That's fine with me," Sabina told the child.

"OK;" Xea's head slowly bobbed as she carefully considered the offer of a different home. "I want Kat to live wiff me. No baby!" Her face tightened into an angry scowl, "And NO mommy!"

● ● ●

Mia panted with lusty arousal. They were together again!

Nick excitedly stripped off her clothes. His fervent blue eyes glinted in the dim living quarters adjacent to the Cotton Room.

Mia wrapped her arms around his neck, "This is absolutely the last time."

"You're not thinking of that idiot Jake again?" the naked man mocked.

Mia nodded, "He's going to emerge tomorrow."

She trembled with ecstasy.

Nick's hands slid seductively down her bare body, "So this will be one last time to forever remember me by."

• • •

"This is going to be a problem," Floyd muttered to himself as he slouched on the rustic canvas easy chair in the beach hut. The cat looked up at the mumbling man before returning to the early evening nap.

Another new image of a fabulously intricate space suit appeared in the engineer's head, the seventh in just the last hour, he realized. There must be dozens, or perhaps hundreds of excellent designs that the Master/Minion could show him.

He would soon have to stop for the night but a good engineer would eventually have to muddle through all of the available options.

• • •

Mia stopped the tedious work of freeing the still slumbering Jake from the cocoon and pressed her stubby fingers against her throbbing brow. She had a particularly nasty headache and, she lamented, a huge amount of remorse after last night's final fling with Nick. Since she'd begun the laborious extraction process many hours ago, Mia had mercilessly lambasted herself about the carnal misadventure with the alluring cad. The woman was sure that the stress of the secret erotic escapade would soon cause her to be ill.

She sighed heavily and studied the slim sleeping man: the sparse hair on his chest, his angular facial features and the crazily splayed black hair on his head. Jake could never be the fiery sexual trophy that Nick was, she realized. Mia stroked his warm round shoulders. Her fingers wandered across his chest to his neck and slowly up to cup his sleeping face. He looked so tranquil and untroubled.

The heavy weight of shame tugged her miserably downward. "You must never know how I have betrayed you," she whispered. Mia leaned forward and delicately kissed his temple, "I will forever strive to be your perfect mate.

Jake 2.2+ slowly opened his eyes. His big brown puppy dog eyes, Mia noticed. A warm and adoring smile spread slowly across his face.

"Mmm," he haltingly whispered, "Maaa...Mia?"

A dry quivering queasiness spread through the woman's chest, "Yes my love?"

He gasped and cleared his throat, "It...it's so good to...to see you."

Mia gasped in anguish as the emotional upheaval proved to be too much for her to bear. She collapsed on man's chest in a full out wail of agony.

Jake's unsteady hand came up and stroked the hysterical

woman's back.

He sobbed along with her, "I..I missed you...so much!"

• • •

"You definitely did it," Sabina noted as she inspected the four new space suits laid out on the massive plank worktable in the Fabricator Room. With a smug grin, she turned to Floyd and added, "Or should I say that your little robot buddies did it?" She hoisted one of the helmets and picked appraisingly at the spongy black seal that encircled the opening.

"It was a group effort," Floyd chuckled.

The woman's face grew solemn as she stared into the tall man's eyes, "When can I get out of here? Ever since Jake emerged three months ago and shacked up with Mia in that disgustingly saccharin love nest in the Cotton Room, I just can't stand this place anymore."

Sabina's venomous bashing of her ex-lover unnerved Floyd. "Fairly soon, I guess. The preparations have taken much longer than I thought. It took two days to make that pocket watch of mine and two months to put together the space suits."

She set the helmet aside and fiddled with the assortment of valves and tubes that adorned the front of the grayish garments, "Why so long, oh great master of Minions?"

"It wasn't the robots," Floyd ruefully admitted, "I discovered that the Master/Minion had detailed descriptions of over four hundred different types of pressure suits that were in use from 1958 until 3061." His hand glided lovingly over the crisp new fabric, "I spent *way* too much time studying the most advanced suit designs which were so complex that we undoubtedly would not be able to use them. Marie eventually told me to just pick something from our era."

The engineer proudly held up the smallest of the four suits, "May I present, custom built for Sabina Jackson Finney of San Francisco, this splendid 'Mark 9 Low Earth Orbit Protective Garment' circa 2065, complete with air reprocessing and active cooling."

Sabina rolled her eyes.

"The stylish matching boots are extra, by the way," Floyd added. "I had to come up with a space suit design that Old Floyd could eventually wear on the surface of the Cerces, if he figures out how to get out there."

She scrutinized the sturdy footwear; "Osman told me that he and Old Mia are going to tend to little Xea in the Rocky Mountain Camp for a few weeks after the baby is born."

"Xea's already there with Old Mia. At the rate things are going, she might be there for months," Floyd noted. "Apparently Ynez is exhausted from the difficult pregnancy and her demanding and sometimes spiteful daughter. Marie thinks that she's probably anemic and prescribed extended bed rest after the birth."

"What about Old Floyd?" Sabina asked with some annoyance. "Why can't the dallying daddy-to-be help out with his spawn?"

Floyd grimaced at the indictment of his older twin, "Officially Old Floyd will be exploring the Outer Causeway after the baby's birth, but between you and I, Old Floyd and Ynez are reliving the same difficulties that have plagued that relationship for many millennia."

He shook his head sadly, "She can't offer him enough mental stimulation and so he spends progressively more time working on other more interesting things. He's never around to enjoy the little moments with her, so she resents all of the time that he spends on his various projects."

The usually flippant woman followed the dismal assessment with consternation. Perhaps, Floyd surmised, because of the recent spectacular failure of her protracted partnership with Jake. "Hopefully the baby will satisfy Ynez's need for intimacy."

She considered his opinion at length before answering. "Floyd clones can be *such* bastards," Sabina declared with a strange mixture of scorn and awe. She stared at him with a dark and penetrating look of appraisal for an uncomfortably long time.

The woman's face eventually softened to merely a slightly menacing smile, "So when do I get out of here?"

"I think that we can start the trek to Realm 3 in two days. Old Floyd is going to travel with us for part of the journey to get a feel for the new equipment and to map part of the Outer Causeway." Floyd realized that the intense conversation with the fervent artist had caused him the sweat profusely.

A Minion Robot pushed through the stretchy slit of the

aperture door and floated past the array of manufacturing equipment that filled the Fabricator Room. The robot nudged Sabina aside and came to rest in front of Floyd.

The petite redhead glared at the insolent machine.

"Floyd?" the Minion inquired in Marie's lilting voice.

"Yeah; what is it dear?"

"Ynez has gone into labor," the doctor reported, "I'm guessing that the baby will be born in about a half an hour. You and Sabina should join us at the cottage in the Southwest Desert."

"Alright; we're on our way."

They left the Fabricator Room and strolled though the tunnel towards the Desert habitat.

"Well this time it seems to be much calmer than when Xea was born," Sabina mused.

Floyd smiled nostalgically as they walked, "Just before she was born, Marie and I were being secretly stalked by the Minion Robots."

The woman laughed, "Yes. I recall that you two had snuck off to swim in the Water Supply Tank."

They stepped through the aperture and into the sweltering desert.

"A Minion Robot reeled Marie in by her ankle when she tried to swim away," Floyd recalled, "and we ended up sprinting here in our swimsuits."

They joined Osman and Jake on the small flagstone patio just outside of the little white adobe.

Twenty minutes later Marie and Mia delivered the second baby to be born in the Realm. His proud parents promptly named the placid dark haired boy Tinsley 0.1, whimsically attaching the made-up version and sequence numbers to the little one's name as they had done with Xea.

6. The Outer Causeway

"How's that new space suit working?" Floyd asked Sabina as the three travelers bounded along in the diminished gravity down the long corridor.

"I suppose that it's acceptable," the woman puffed. "It has a strange smell that reminds me of cantaloupes and the hissing of the air reprocessor is driving me nutty."

"You'll get used to it," Old Floyd assured her as they slowed for the looming barrier door in the distance.

"I don't know, boys," Sabina grumbled. "This is not my idea of a lavish vacation.

"How's the baby?" Floyd asked his older clone.

"He's doing great. I took him over to the Rocky Mountain Camp yesterday so that he could meet his big sister."

The travelers stopped at the massive gray door for a brief rest.

"What did the precious one think of her new sib?" Sabina asked.

Old Floyd panted in the stiff new space suit as he leaned against the heavy door, "Xea did surprisingly well." He gasped from the strenuous romp; "I let her hold Tinsley for a few minutes."

"I'm sure that was *too* adorable," Sabina said mawkishly.

"It was," he admitted. "Xea has already nicknamed him 'Tin,' which is short for 'Tin-O-One,' she claims."

"Oh; I get it," the younger man interjected, "Tinsley zero point one: Tin-0-1."

"She is a sharp young wag," Sabina mused.

"Tin *is* one of my favorite metals," Old Floyd admitted. "Fortunately she didn't nickname him Praseodymium."

Floyd activated the massive door. Beyond it, stretching far off in either direction, was an unvarying white corridor. "This is the Outer Causeway," he announced.

Sabina scrutinized the passageway, "How do we know which way to go?"

Floyd withdrew a fat black crayon from the pocket of the space suit. The man held the tip to the tunnel wall for several seconds as he reviewed the information that was supplied to him by the Master/Minion. He resolutely drew a stout arrow pointing down one corridor and below it he inscribed 'anti-spinward.' Floyd stepped several paces to the side and produced a second arrow pointing in the opposite direction with the notation 'spinward.' In gigantic letters, he wrote 'Realm 17' between the two arrows.

The engineer returned the crayon to his pocket and turned to face his traveling companions, "If we could look down on the North Pole of the Cerces from high above, we'd see that it rotates counterclockwise like most of the objects that orbit around the sun. Spinward is in the direction of the rotation and anti-spinward is the other way."

Sabina motioned to the impromptu sign, "The Causeway goes all of the way around our beloved detention facility, right?"

The men nodded in unison.

"What difference does it make if we go hither or yon?"

"Well," Floyd sighed, "you and I are traveling to Realm 3. If we travel spinward, we will pass thirteen other Realms along the way. If we head anti-spinward, we pass only five. It will take less than half of the time if we go in right direction."

"The sooner that I can shed this malodorous garment, the better," Sabina groused.

• • •

The space suit clad adventurers parted ways. Old Floyd stood next to the recently created signage at the juncture to Realm 17 for several minutes to watch Floyd and Sabina lope off toward the distant and unknown area that would likely be the woman's home for the foreseeable future.

Before beginning the expedition, the two men had agreed that he would travel spinward and attempt to enter the neighboring Realm which held the dark and dead remains of Kurt's Tribe.

Old Floyd trotted off towards his goal.

After nearly two hours of numbing tedium in the maddeningly uniform white tunnel, he came upon a smooth gray barrier door. As his younger clone had done earlier,

Old Floyd marked the wall opposite the door with two opposing arrows and the place name: 'Realm 16, Kurt's Tribe.'

The old engineer opened the barrier without difficulty and strode through the blue-lit passage. Although still quite weak, the unrelenting tug of gravity discernibly increased as he traveled. He passed through the now irrelevant air lock and entered the airless caverns of Realm 16.

Old Floyd activated his light-disc and directed the amber beam around the menacing stone pinnacles. He now regretted the decision to explore the ghostly and unnerving caverns alone. For a dozen minutes, the man cautiously examined the area within sight of the still open door and the reassuring sapphire light that spilled from it.

Finally he had satisfied himself that these caverns were indistinguishable from the more familiar ones of Realm 17. He leapt mightily across the short distance towards the barrier but quickly stifled a second jump to complete the trip.

What was that?

Old Floyd swiveled around and shone the light back and forth over the craggy surface.

There!

He painstakingly studied the small and oddly colored object. In the oppressively dark cave, where everything was in hues of black and brown, this imperfect sphere was mottled red. Old Floyd crept up to the little thing. He scuffed lightly at it with his boot. It *seemed* harmless.

Old Floyd gently retrieved the item. It was a crudely made toy ball.

Perhaps Marie and Boy X had tossed it to each other thousands of years earlier.

• • •

After leaving Old Floyd behind at the juncture, Sabina and Floyd traveled in silence for nearly an hour, each assured of the others proximity by the sound of persistent panting that emanated from the two-way radio.

"Floyd," Sabina finally called to her traveling companion when she could no long endure the monotony of the trip.

"What is it?"

"I'm sure that you told me at some point," she huffed, "but remind me of whom you were cloned."

"Francis Floyd Bernal," he chuckled. "Technically we are twin brothers, but I always kind of imagined him as my dad."

"I only ever remember you speaking of your Granny Camille, and I think someone called Raina; or some such name."

"Raelene; she was my sister and surrogate mother." Floyd stopped and turned towards her, "Let's take a break for a few minutes." He stretched his arms high above his head and splayed his gloved fingers several times. "Why the sudden interest in ancient history?"

"Boredom I guess," she grinned through the clear domed helmet. "What became of Francis?"

"I never met him. Lieutenant Bernal was in the Army Corps of Engineers during the Amero-Asian War. He was killed in a battle outside of Ulaanbaatar about a year before I was born."

"How did you happen to be cloned from your dead soldier boy brother?"

"Camille and Raelene really adored Francis," a faraway look of remembrance settled on Floyd's face, "There were pictures of him everywhere at Grandma Camille's house in Magdalena. Raelene got a hold of a DNA sample from her big brother and through some sort of special government cloning program, I was produced and implanted in her uterus."

For several minutes they were both lost in thought. Floyd pointed down the hallway and they started off.

"What about you, Sabina?' he wondered. "Who was your genetic originator?"

"Let's not discuss the Finney family fiasco," she evaded.

"No; I told you about my ancestry, now it's your turn."

During the protracted silence, Floyd guessed that there was only a slim chance that Sabina would succumb to his probing regarding her past.

"My dad was the infamous San Francisco architect, Jackson Finney."

He pressed her to continue, "That part I knew."

"Long before I came around, 'Old Daddy Jack' had a condom malfunction with one of his many dimwitted bed mates. Nine months later, a wretched and unwelcome hatchling arrived. The resentful mother named the frail child Naomi. Shortly afterwards the bimbo disappeared forever, leaving Naomi ever after in the faulty care of Jackson Finney. Thirty years later, apparently to assuage some residual guilt that he had about producing an extremely sickly but never the less ingenious daughter, 'Daddy Dearest' had a sample of Naomi's DNA repaired to produce me so that he could make a second feeble attempt at fatherhood."

"You're not at all spiteful about your childhood, are you?" Floyd quipped.

"You wanted to know," she scoffed.

He stopped suddenly and pointed ahead. A barrier door punctuated the inexhaustible white sameness of the tunnel wall. Floyd glanced at the clock affixed to the sleeve of his suit. "A hundred and twenty-nine minutes, it should take about eleven more hours to reach Realm 3."

Sabina pressed the palm of her gloved hand to the face of her helmet in exasperation, "I hope there's a hot tub and a couple of stiff drinks waiting at the Inn at the end of the road."

The engineer marked the wall adjacent to the door and they set off again.

"I don't think that I've told you," Floyd hesitated to

consider the wisdom of the matter that he was about to broach, "but I have always thought that you are the smartest person that I've ever met."

She laughed, "Don't tease me."

"No; really."

"Why in the world would you think that I am so brilliant?"

"It's true, Sabina. Nearly everything that we have or use ultimately trails back to you. I reside in a fantastic Polynesian paradise because five thousand years ago you started work on the Cityscape and proved to the rest of the group what a great idea it would be to live in a themed habitat."

"One good idea does not a genius make," she wryly noted.

Floyd struggled for another convincing example; "During the three years that passed before you were first cloned by the Cotton, the six of us were barely able to attire ourselves in a few tattered remnants of blue fabric. Within a week of your arrival, you had fabricated much more practical and stylish clothing."

"I didn't want to wear those hideous blue togas that you had concocted," she confessed.

"But those are just two of hundreds of examples. You are a remarkably creative and industrious woman," he fawned.

Sabina tugged tersely on his arm and firmly pressed him back against the wall. She stared through the thick helmet faceplate at him. "No; you're wrong," she whispered. "I realized long ago that working with you and Nick made me a much better artist than I would ever have managed on my own."

Floyd studied the woman's troubled face, she seemed surprisingly self-conscious.

From across the few inches that physically separated them, he could now sense the vast and daunting distance that had, until now, protected her from the oppressive misconception that she had of herself.

"I would *never* deceive you about your well-earned talents," Floyd declared.

7. Realm Three

They traveled in silence for hours through the long tunnel.

Floyd dearly hoped that his painful prodding of Sabina's psyche would not harm their long friendship.

During a short pause that they made to mark one of the Realm entrances, Floyd had surreptitiously glanced sideways at her while she waited. Sabina's face was puffy and red. Isolated in the clear space suit helmet that prevented her hands from wiping them away, thin streams of tears still marked her cheeks.

They plodded on.

"*You bastard*," she finally muttered.

"I'm so sorry, I should never have..."

She sniffled, "Sometimes you're just such a jerk."

The woman sighed woefully.

"The truth is," she rasped, "I've always been in awe of you, Floyd. Even though we could never seem to stay together for very long as lovers, I always hoped that eventually we'd work things out."

Floyd listened with an unusual mix of apprehension and delight. He had eagerly engaged in their many brief and sporadic dalliances in the past but only recently had his amorous interests abruptly changed forever.

"I knew that I'd lost any claim to you on that sad day that you brought the flawless Doctor Marie to the Cityscape for the first time," Sabina lamented. "You slipped your arm around her waist and had a stupid moonstruck smile." She moaned with defeat, "It seemed that I would evermore be stuck with the half-witted Jake."

"What exactly was the attraction between you and Jake?" he wondered.

"He was surprisingly compliant in the boudoir," she snickered, "and he was in utter fear of me, so he never questioned any unsavory behavior on my part."

"Here it is," Floyd stopped, "Realm 3."

The weary travelers gawked at the long-sought portal that was indistinguishable from the many others that they had passed during the drawn-out expedition. They ventured through the door and down the long passageway to the airlock. While they waited for the chamber to adjust the pressure between the different environments, Floyd fidgeted with a seemly trivial flat metal cylinder that dangled from his tool belt. The device resembled an old-fashioned tuna fish can but was actually a deceptively simple air pressure gauge. He stared at the stiff indicator needle that was affixed to one face of the device. In the hospitable environment of the Beach Habitat, the pointer had been parallel to the face of the instrument. During the tedious trip through the airless tunnel, the needle had deflected decidedly downward to indicate a strong vacuum in the passageway.

Floyd grinned nervously at Sabina as they waited; he had intentionally not told her that they would be forced to trudge back to Realm 17 if the ambient air pressure beyond the airlock was insufficient.

The needle crept slowly upward.

Two weeks earlier, Floyd had instructed the Master/Minion to adjust the temperature and air pressure to standard levels but he had since endured several troubling nightmares about suffocating in the mysterious new region.

When the outer door slowly rumbled open, the indicator was again parallel with the face of the instrument. Floyd endeavored to double-check the pressure measurement. He retrieved a small clear jar from a pouch attached to the warm thermal exhaust vent of his suit. He and Old Floyd had used the same tightly sealed container many times before to appraise the atmospheric conditions beyond other airlocks. He sloshed the water about in the airtight jar. The fluid did not freeze; therefore, Floyd concluded, the surrounding temperature would at least be bearable. He opened the jar and keenly studied the clear liquid; a few tiny bubbles erupted before the water became placid. The air pressure was indeed acceptable.

He covered the jar and returned it to the pouch.

Sabina had watched the tests with concern, "What are you doing?"

He unfastened his helmet, "Just checking the local conditions." Floyd wriggled his nose as he drew a deep breath in the long uninhabited world. It was brisk with a faint smell of ozone but otherwise satisfactory.

They struggled out of their stiff suits. They took turns

relieving themselves behind a nearby boulder and dined in bleary silence on a long-delayed meal. As Floyd carefully stowed the space suits near the barrier door, Sabina laid out the two bedrolls. Within several minutes of crawling into them, they both slept.

• • •

"It should be right around here," Floyd called hopefully across the dark void to her.

All that he could see of her was a distant beam of yellow light slowly brushing over the rocky formations of the cavern. Guided by an imperfect mental map supplied by the Master/Minion that floated hazily in Floyd's head, they had spent most of the morning trudging around in search of the elusive aperture door that would lead them into the Realm.

Sabina's spotlight stopped suddenly, "I've found the coveted entryway to the kingdom."

He trotted to her side.

As Sabina illuminated the area, Floyd spread the edges of the stretchy membrane that made up the slit of the door. A resilient white panel beyond obstructed the gap. He tapped appraisingly on the material. It didn't seem particularly sturdy. Floyd balled up his fist and walloped the thin sheet, which produced a ragged hole. After several more blows enlarged the opening, Sabina peered through the rend.

"It's a dark tunnel," she reported.

The woman stepped into the passageway and tapped at her light-disc pendent. The long-unused ceiling lights shimmered weirdly before steadying to a faint cobalt blue.

Floyd pushed the two bundles of supplies through the opening and joined her.

For nearly an hour they traveled cautiously down the shadowy tunnel, stopping at the infrequently spaced aperture doors to briefly investigate each room. One door led to a dark storehouse of assorted materials, similar but much smaller than the vast repository in their own world. Several doors concealed the primitive and startlingly well-preserved living quarters of the long-gone residents.

Sabina ventured into one particularly interesting chamber while Floyd waited at the door. She idly examined several crude tools made of odd brownish pipe with irregular lumps of fractured metal lashed to them.

She scornfully held up one especially misshapen implement, "Apparently a robotic caveman cobbled together a prehistoric ax from remnants of an old Chevy."

They continued on.

"I'm going to leave you here in two days," Floyd mentioned as they searched the blue-lit passage for the Cotton Room.

"I know," she glanced up at him with a half smile. "I can manage on my own, you silly boy."

The tunnel lighting flickered to life some distance ahead of them. Suspended against the wall were two hibernating Minion Robots. The explorers stopped to examine the quiescent sentinels.

"These are the first Minions that I've seen in days," the

engineer noted.

The woman poked at one of the dormant machines, "This one is rather unique."

Floyd compared the two robots. One was indistinguishable from every other Minion that he had ever seen; the other was almost entirely black.

"Pick one," he urged.

"Why?" she frowned.

"I've been thinking about this for several days, I'd like you to keep a Minion Robot close at hand for communication purposes and personal safety."

"Personal safety?" she scowled.

"Ignoring any problems that you might eventually have with Jasper, breaking a leg while you're alone in this Realm would likely prove to be fatal," Floyd sternly noted.

"Mmm; I guess you're right." Sabina drummed her fingers on the side of the black robot, "This one."

"I thought so," he clutched the sides of the idle machine. "Activate this Minion Robot," Floyd spoke out loud more as a show for the woman than anything else.

The faint red indicator light blinked several times and the ebony machine bobbed slightly as it energized.

"Your sole duties will be to accompany Sabina 6.37 at all times and respond promptly to her demands."

She brushed the accumulated dust of many centuries from the stately black servant. "He reminds me of an acquiescent old butler that was in the service of my father," a mischievous smile crossed her face. "In honor of the old steward, I shall call him Sebastian."

• • •

While Sabina and her docile mechanical roommate investigated the modest Cotton Room and the adjoining living quarters, Floyd appraised the condition of the huge dormant mound of thin silvery fibers. After thousands of years of speculating about the enigmatic substance, the group had learned only recently that the Cotton was an intricate biorobotic organism that the Master/Minion directed to duplicate various life forms. Now as one of the two new human overseers of the immense robotic space ship, he was about to command the Master/Minion to use this very mound to produce a human clone for the first time.

In the now familiar mental process, he summoned the attention of the Master/Minion. Floyd careful phrased his request to avoid any ambiguity, "Produce a single Human Test Subject known as Jasper version 1 using the biorobotic cloning interface in Test Area 3."

The Mater/Minion acknowledged his dictate.

Floyd watched with some apprehension as the gray threads wriggled together to form a large and still very vague cocoon.

8. The workaday world

Floyd wearily observed that it was midday in the Hawaiian Beach Habitat as he stepped through the aperture door. He was particularly groggy and sore from the numbingly long journey home from Realm 3. He stood feebly at the entrance to allow his eyes to adjust to the bright noontime glare. The rumble and crash of faraway surf and the rich sweet smell of the breakers reminded him of why he dearly loved this place. And Marie; he corrected the list of cherished attributes, most importantly Marie was here.

He shuffled weakly into the shelter.

Marie set down the bowl of food and stared in surprise at the exhausted man for several seconds. A huge grin stretched across her face, "Welcome back, Mr. Bernal." She embraced the languid and sweaty traveler. "Would you like to eat or sleep first?"

"I need something to drink," Floyd whispered hoarsely.

The woman led him to the canvas easy chair and filled a white mug with water. Floyd drained the container and held it out for replenishment. She obliged him with a refill.

The man's color and disposition improved.

Marie kissed him softly on the forehead.

"That was a grueling trip," he finally declared.

She sprinkled additional morsels into the bowl of food and offered it to the man.

"Thanks." He sampled the meal, "It took nearly thirteen hours of tedious trotting. It was *so* dull."

Marie nodded in sympathy, "I saw Old Floyd just after he returned from the caverns in Kurt's world and he said the same thing." She strolled to the sturdy brown table against the back wall and then returned to him with her hands tightly cupped together, "He brought a memento back for me."

The woman opened her hands to reveal a misshapen red ball.

Floyd studied the strange plaything, "It looks like a little round bean bag."

"Boy X, uh," she corrected herself, "Ben and I played a silly game with this ball in the scant gravity near the barrier door." Marie squeezed the soft object several times before tossing it back to the brown table. "Tell me about Realm 3, my love."

He dropped a handful of colorful tidbits into his mouth, "It's much smaller than our world. The former residents apparently barely progressed beyond the caveman stage. There was a startling lack of any type of advanced technology."

Marie handed him a spoon and a second bowl filled with pungent brown Sobaco, "How's Sabina?"

Floyd frowned at the mention of the woman, "She did well once we got to Realm 3." The worn-out look returned to his face, "During the trip, I inadvertently discovered that our pretentious and innovative friend suffers from an appallingly severe inferiority complex."

"Really?" The doctor considered the revelation; "I remember some spare scraps from a Clinical Psychology class in Med school." She pondered the nearly forgotten college course, "Often those suffering from feelings of inadequacy overcompensate with aggressive behavior and the all consuming production of transcending creations."

"Arrogance and endless attention to artistic detail, that would certainly describe Sabina." Floyd slurped the last of the smelly brown paste from the bowl, "What's been going on here?"

Marie's eyebrows arched up, "Mia's pregnant."

Floyd smiled knowingly, "Well; with all of the lovemaking since Jake's return..."

"No;" Marie held her hand up to stop him, "I did a prenatal exam on her and everything seemed rather standard for a first time mom. But to satisfy my own curiosity about the baby's gender, I used the Master/Minion to probe the tiny tot's particulars."

He tipped his head in confusion about the implied intrigue, "So boy or girl?"

"It's a girl, but that's not important," the doctor's face darkened. "Nick is the father, not Jake."

Floyd winced, "I was afraid of that, does anyone else know about it?"

Marie shook her head, "I think that Mia suspects, but

neither of the men have any idea."

He considered the perilous news, "We can't tell anyone about this, Marie. The stability of our little group could easily be destroyed by an episode of jealousy and sexual deceit." Floyd scowled, "Unfortunately this sort of thing has happened in the past."

"I agree," she nodded.

Floyd felt suddenly very tired, the long journey and transgressions of others drained him of any remaining strength. He studied the pensive doctor; she was deep in thought, no doubt about the unseemly consequences that might yet befall them from the infidelity.

Marie closed her eyes, "Time will tell what damage this impropriety will bring."

• • •

It was midmorning in the Southwest Desert Habitat and the family was tending to various matters on the patio.

Xea had at last matured enough to tolerate the brief daily lessons that all four-year-olds should receive, Ynez reflected as she tutored her daughter.

The little girl fidgeted with the sheet of white paper at the dining table as she painstaking scratched out her name in huge wobbly letters.

"Very good," Ynez admired the work. "Alright; let's do some language work."

The girl groaned before she recited the much-practiced phrase in English, *"The cat is my best friend."*

Xea tipped her head in thought before she continued, *"Neko wa watashi no shin'yudesu."*

"Excellent pronunciation," the woman praised, "Japanese is difficult to speak properly but you did it quite well. Now the same phrase in Spanish, please."

The girl pouted at the burdensome extra workload, *"El gato es mi amigo mejor."*

Ynez glanced at Old Floyd as he watched the tutorial from the canvas armchair. The man nodded affirmatively at his daughter's correct rendition.

The woman smiled, "Daddy says that you did it right."

"Le chat est mon meilleur ami," Xea waggishly declared.

Ynez stared at her daughter in surprise. Old Floyd set aside the journal at the unexpected rendition.

"Was that French?" Ynez inquired.

"Oui, maman," the girl proudly acknowledged.

"Where did you learn that?"

"Osman taught it to me when I lived at the Rocky Mountain Camp," Xea stated matter-of-factly.

Ynez's brow furrowed with dismay. She turned to Old Floyd and whispered in despair, "I thought that it was decided that I would be the *only* teacher in our group."

He shrugged at his unduly demoralized mate, "Think of it as an exclusive French Canadian boarding school." Old Floyd still felt surprisingly guilty about the protracted exile that his spirited daughter had been forced to endure in the Rocky Mountain Camp on behalf of Ynez.

Tin began to cry in the house as he awoke from his midmorning nap. Ynez stood stiffly in a melancholy stupor for several seconds before she shuffled into the cottage to tend to the toddler.

Old Floyd watched the moody woman with concern, Marie had told him months ago that Ynez was suffering through a particularly troubling bout of postpartum blues.

"Can I play now, Daddy?" the perky little girl asked.

"May I play now," he absently corrected. "Yes you may."

Xea sprang from the chair and skipped off to the toy box. She sorted through the vast collection of handmade playthings. "This stuff isn't fun anymore!" the pint-sized pixie declared as she frowned at the trove of toys.

Xea pressed her hand to her chin. "I know what I want." For nearly a minute the girl stood transfixed in thought.

With a big grin, she stood and twirled around several times before she crooned a song that Ynez had taught her weeks earlier, "*I hear the sound of her gentle words,*" she curtsied to her father, "*on the wind that lifts her perfume though the air. I'm pickin' up good vibrations, she's givin' me excitations.*" The tune trailed off when the petite songstresses could recall no further lyrics.

Old Floyd applauded, "Very nice, my dear."

Xea hugged her father. "Don't tell mom," she confessed, "but I know how to say the phrase another way too. Do you want to hear it?"

"Sure."

"*Kuu tong rwaw katze hao.*"

"Is that Swahili?" the man wondered.

"Sa-whaty?" Xea's face twisted comically with incomprehension, "No, Dad. It's called '*rEn sprak*,' which means 'People Speak'."

"Who taught you that?"

She rolled her eyes, "The Master/Minion of course! It's the way that *everyone* talked when the Cerces was built."

She trotted off and danced euphorically around on the warm flagstones.

"I suppose that makes sense," the old engineer muttered. "Of course the speech of mankind would have changed over a thousand years."

He watched his daughter's impromptu rhythmic extravaganza.

The warm bucolic illusion was dashed by the abrupt appearance of a Minion Robot. Old Floyd scrutinized the machine as it darted towards his daughter. The robot stopped just short of the girl and daintily placed an intricately fashioned replica of a miniature horse on the patio.

Xea sighed in dismay, "You were *supposed* to bring two of them, you stupid doodlebot!"

The inept mechanized courier scurried away.

With the departure of the robot, Ynez joined Old Floyd on the patio. The two startled parents stared with consternation at the child as she retrieved the figurine from the flagstones.

"Xea; what just happened here with the Minion Robot?" Old Floyd asked the girl.

She looked up lightheartedly at her father as she grasped the equine curio, "I wanted to play with the two horses that Old Auntie Mia has in the Rocky Mountain Camp and so I sent a robot dum-dum to get them."

"You sent a robot to get them," the man slowly repeated.

The girl nodded proudly, "They do whatever I tell them to do, Daddy."

• • •

The placid reverberations of the nearby breakers belied the unhappy proceedings in the beach shelter.

"Old Mia did get fairly banged up by the marauding Minion messenger," Marie advised Old Floyd and Ynez. "She has several nasty bruises and two dreadful lacerations, one of which took ten stitches to close up."

"I hope she'll be alright," Old Floyd winced.

"She's in her late sixties," Marie noted, "with the joint problems and protracted recovery time that most senior citizens face. It's just much better for them if they can avoid any unnecessary trauma."

Xea whimpered remorsefully in the corner of the hut as the adults discussed her unseemly commandeering of the robot.

Ynez shook her head sadly.

"What exactly can we do to prevent this sort of thing from happening again?" the man asked.

Marie thought for several seconds, "Floyd and I could sever her link to the Master/Minion. That would certainly prevent any future misdeeds."

Old Floyd scowled at the suggestion, "That seems too extreme. She *has* stumbled upon some interesting new information recently with the help of the Master/Minion."

Marie studied her distraught niece; "We could instruct the Master/Minion to block Xea from commanding the robots. To be on the safe side, perhaps we should consider restricting everything except information retrieval." The doctor chuckled, "That way, we won't risk having the Cerces suddenly fall out of orbit and plunge into the sun if Xea has a temper tantrum."

Old Floyd grinned at the unexpected levity, "I think that's a wise suggestion."

Ynez grimly followed the debate. "OK; that seems like an

appropriate punishment," she nodded.

Marie dispassionately studied the melancholy woman; she quickly summoned the current telemetric medical information about her friend that was constantly being updated by the Master/Minion from all of the Human Test Subjects aboard the spacecraft. Ynez had a peculiar chemical imbalance in her brain that would require significant investigation in the future.

"Marie?" Old Floyd called to the distracted doctor.

The tall dark haired woman blinked several times, "Sorry, I was thinking about something else." She glanced at the glum girl, "Since I will be imposing the punishment upon Xea, I think that I should be the one who delivers the bad news to her."

Ynez and Old Floyd nodded.

"Why don't you two take a short walk on the beach while I carry out the execution."

"Be gentle," the man teased as they departed.

Marie watched the couple shuffle across the black dunes.

She grimaced; as a physician, Marie had delivered bad news to children many times in the past, but never to a close relative and certainly not to anyone as unique as her sparkly and inquisitive niece.

The woman sat on the canvas easy chair and beckoned the contrite child to join her. The weepy girl plodded achingly across the floor and stared sadly at her revered aunt.

Marie wrapped her arms around the pitiful youngster, "You know what you did was wrong."

Xea nodded ruefully.

"You are a very gifted young lady," Marie proclaimed. "But sadly, you can't be trusted with this particular talent."

The girl flinched as the woman raked at the emotional wound.

"From this day on," the Marie declared, "your interactions with the Master/Minion and the robots will be restricted to communication and information gathering only."

Xea burst into tears.

9. The 30 Gigahertz Array

Floyd's back ached from three restless nights on a thin mat on the floor of the sparse Cotton Room in Realm 3. After several laborious days of dragging heavy provisions around the Realm for Sabina, he dearly looked forward to returning tonight to the comfortable bed that he shared with Marie in the far off Hawaiian Beach Habitat. Four days ago, he had plodded alone nearly a third of the way around the Cerces to deliver an overly large bundle of hard-to-find supplies for Sabina.

Sabina's head popped through the slit of the aperture door from her sleeping quarters. A wide grin stretched across her lively and angular face, "I have to admit that I've really enjoyed having you here, Floyd." She stepped into the room with a large bowl of the familiar dry food that Floyd had brought for her. "You're much better company than my loquacious friend Sebastian," she scoffed as she passed by the idle robot.

The man grimaced as he arched his sore back. "The Master/ Minion says that the Cotton will release Jasper from his cocoon in about twelve hours," he noted. "By then I hope to be nearly back to the caverns in Realm 17. I'm still very uneasy about leaving you alone with him."

"Not to worry, my overly protective friend." She handed him the bowl and gnawed on her lower lip as she silently considered a more difficult issue. "I want you to allow Sebastian and me to kill Jasper if things get wildly out of control."

Floyd was unsettled by the alarming nature of the request,

"Well; I don't...."

She stared at him with an unusually pleading look of vulnerability.

Floyd reconsidered her request. "OK. If, in your excellent judgment, you decide that it's necessary, you or any of the local Minions may kill off Jasper."

She solemnly nodded, "Thank you."

"Remember, though," he admonished, "there are frighteningly few humans left. If we're ever going to rebuild our species, we'll need every single available individual regardless of any minor misbehavior."

"You're right, of course." A sly grin emerged, "Before you leave for the hinterlands, let me show you one of my especially grand new creations."

After finishing the light meal, they traveled down the tunnel trailed by the ever-present black robot. The artist and her entourage squeezed though an aperture door and into a dark room. Sabina tapped on her light-disc pendent and the sparse local illumination flickered on above their heads.

It was a boulder-strewn warehouse, Floyd observed. He could discern the beginnings of several orderly stone pathways and some thick rock walls. Ever busy and endlessly creative, he mused, Sabina was apparently fashioning a complex new habitat.

With her arms held out pretentiously, as if declaring it to the very gods themselves, she announced, "This is the Empire of Threesia."

"Threesia?" Floyd frowned.

"The third Realm. Threesia. It's not *that* difficult to figure out, you dolt," she rolled her eyes. "Eventually there will be a castle with a dragon infested moat and a splendid green meadow beyond." With an impish smile, she added, "Perhaps several brawny knights astride white stallions will battle to woo the Empress of the Realm."

They wandered amongst the stout stone ramparts and vast rock piles. Floyd carefully examined a huge and orderly wall assembled from thousands of massive boulders. He stared appraisingly at the dainty woman, "I'm impressed by your ability to stack heavy objects."

She laughed, "My robotic roustabout does the heavy work. I just point and shout."

"Wait a minute," Floyd said in sudden irritation, "Sebastian hauled all of these stones around for you?"

"Of course," she shrugged, "I can't lift those things."

"Why did I just spend several days schlepping supplies around the Realm for you?"

"Because you're a great guy," she grinned guilefully.

They returned to the Cotton Room and Floyd gathered his few belongings for the long trip home.

Sabina lugged a bulky hooded robe into the room from her quarters, "Remind me again about what you know of my impending house guest."

"Well; let's see," the man scratched his head as he recalled Marie's past descriptions of Jasper, "he's tall and stocky with reddish-brown hair, so you two will have that in common. Ah, he's Australian and apparently has some knowledge of archaic weaponry." Floyd's eyes narrowed with alarm, "Marie says that he will single-mindedly pursue assigned objectives. I suspect that he'd be a great assassin or divorce lawyer."

Sabina followed the description carefully.

"Evidently Jasper and Marie were 'mates,' although I'm not sure if that's an Aussie euphemism for lovers or just friends."

"Are we just a tiny bit jealous that our girlfriend has a past?" Sabina chortled.

"A little," Floyd blushed.

He hoisted his sack of belonging and hugged the small woman. "Are you sure that you can handle Jasper?" Floyd asked her with concern. "Marie says that he can be quite forceful and aggressive at times."

"Not to worry, my overly protective friend," she sneered fiendishly. "I have concocted a ingenious plan to put poor helpless Jasper forever in his place as my subservient underling."

Floyd's brow arched up as he considered the innovative and strong-willed woman. "I bet you have."

• • •

Far to the spinward side of the Cerces 4, back in the area known as Realm 17 by Floyd and the others, Xea clattered out onto the flagstone patio of her little house with her tall middle-aged father.

"What shall we play, daddy?" Xea galloped about with bouncy energy.

"I don't know, sweet pea," the man said.

With an exhausted and despondent stare, Ynez watched the man and the girl cheerfully socialize through the open door of the house before she gathered up her drowsy one-year-old son. The woman lay down on the rustic bed that dominated the small cottage and nestled with the acquiescent toddler for a long over due afternoon nap. Outside she could hear the boisterous sounds of her estranged mate and daughter as they played.

"One, two, three, GO!" Xea shouted.

Old Floyd catapulted the girl high into the air before he caught the pint-sized aviatrix.

The girl giggled as her father snatched her from the sky.

"Again!" Xea implored.

Old Floyd flung his daughter upward.

"Again!"

"This is the last time, sweetie," Old Floyd puffed. He hurled her up, retrieved the plummeting girl and then set her gently down on the warm flagstones."

"That was *so* fun, daddy!" Xea wrapped her arms around her father's legs.

Old Floyd collapsed on the canvas easy chair. "I've got to sit down for a few minutes," he panted in the sweltering afternoon air.

Xea clambered up to join her reclined father, "Daddy; what's a library?"

"A library," Old Floyd slowly said with a faraway look in his eyes, "it's a place where old books are stored. I remember going to the old public library in Socorro when I was about six or seven years old with my Grandma Camille. They had thousands of *real* books there stored on long metal shelves."

Xea tilted her head in bewilderment.

"Why do you want to know about libraries?"

Xea frowned, "The Master/Minion has a library but it doesn't have any books in it."

"Really?" The old engineer's interest was aroused by the girl's declaration. "Tell me about this library."

The girl stared off into the distance as she considered the newly discovered storehouse of information. "It's not a *real* place. There are lots of pictures and sounds." Xea tapped her finger against her cheek several times, "When you want to know about something, the Master/Minion lets you find out about it there."

"Mmm, some sort of research database," Old Floyd

speculated. "What's it called?"

A slow grin crossed Xea's face, "The Library of All Human Knowledge."

"Really?" he considered the startling implications of the discovery. If his first-born had actually stumbled upon the accumulated information and experiences of humanity, they had both the burden and the opportunity to utilize that knowledge.

He resolved to test his daughter's claim.

"Xea; can you find something for me in the library?"

She nodded in earnest.

The engineer carefully selected a piece of complex information that he knew well but she would not be able to guess without assistance. "What is Avogadro's number, my dear?"

Xea blinked several times, "6 dot 023 and a 'x,' then 10 with a little 23 floating above it."

He imagined the numbers as she had reported them, "6.023 x 10 ^{23}, that's right!" It seemed unlikely that she could have made it up.

"What was the name of the king of the fairies in Shakespeare's *A Midsummer Night's Dream*?"

"Shakespeare? What's a Shakespeare?" she stared at him questioningly.

"William Shakespeare wrote stories long ago," he coaxed.

"Ob...Oberon," Xea stammered.

"You're right, sweetheart." Old Floyd quickly considered several persistent questions that he'd pondered recently. "How does our Master/Minion talk to others who are very far away?"

"I don't think that this is right," Xea pouted. She pressed her black eyes closed for several seconds. "There's a big thingy outside that the Master/Minion uses to talk."

"What is it called?"

The girl blinked, "It's like that radio that you made and it's called the 30 Gigahertz Array."

"Thanks honey," Old Floyd hugged his daughter and contemplated the astonishing new discoveries that she had revealed to him. Somewhere on the surface of the Cerces 4 there was probably an immense group of microwave antennas and hidden within the Master/Minion was a repository of the accumulated knowledge of his nearly extinct species.

• • •

Sabina snickered as she completed the preparations for the grand entrance or the grand rescue, depending on your point of view. After toiling for hours to strip the cocoon from most of Jasper's naked and unconscious body, she had instructed Sebastian to remove the remaining silvery matting from the man's face when he began to stir. Her plan was wickedly designed to demonstrate who was the all-powerful master of the Realm.

She donned her elaborate garbs and adjusted the room illumination to a sinister dusky gloom. Sabina watched from the shadows as the robot harshly stripped the remaining fibrous material from the man's face. She cringed as the work progressed; the rough treatment reminded her of bandages being yanked from tender skin. The still unconscious man flinched from the severe handling. Tiny yelps of distress followed each swift movement of the gruff mechanical nursemaid.

Jasper's eyes sprang open in terror.

Just has Sabina had instructed, Sebastian slowly drew two of its serrated appendages towards the man's quivering face, a sputtering arc of high voltage danced menacingly between the metal arms.

The big man screeched and wet himself.

The moment had arrived.

She sprang out of the shadows cloaked in the dark hooded robe, her face was carefully hidden behind a gauzy black wrap. Her outstretched hands clapped together like a single deafening drum beat of crackling thunder.

The Minion ceased the contrived attack and turned to face the cloaked figure. The trembling man glanced at his black shrouded savior.

With the melodramatic flare of a seasoned stage performer, she slowly pointed a single slightly bent finger at the robot.

The black machine obligingly disengaged from the man and floated to her side like a well-trained guard dog. The mysterious master stroked the obedient servant. She slowly swaggered toward the shivering man.

Her hand clamped tightly around his testicles, momentarily driving her sharp nails into his delicate flesh. He winced submissively.

"PLEASE!..Don't kill me!" the trembling man begged.

Satisfied that her intimidating power play had forever established her dominance over the big man, she released him. The woman slowly drew back the hood and wrap to reveal her stern face.

"I am Sabina," she slowly growled, "Empress of the Vast Realm of Threesia, Master of the Formidable Minion Armies and Grand Executioner of Unworthy Subjects."

She drew uncomfortably close to the frightened man's face, "Why do I find you muddling about in my antechamber?"

"I...I don't know...Your Majesty," Jasper clasped his eyes shut in deference to the apparent monarch, "I swear that just a moment ago I was in the University Hospital in Queensland."

She motioned to the waiting robot, "I shall have Sebastian, my obedient mechanized guardian, toss you like the rubbish that you are into the fiery Pit of Turmoil for your trespasses."

"Spare me!" he pleaded.

Excellent; Sabina thought, the clever ruse had apparently cowed the potentially dangerous man into submission.

The petite woman stomped away in mock disgust; "Very well! You may live for now as my meek slave."

She did not want to overplay her hand, she mused. If he demonstrated acceptable behavior in the next few days, hopefully she could allow the handsome man into her bedchamber.

10. The Library of All Human Knowledge

Mia frowned as she hunched over the large journal that she'd used for thousands of years to chronicle the routine and sometimes unusual events that transpired in the Realm.

Over the past four years it had become quite a chore to keep up the records.

She carefully noted the most recent milestone: Xea 0.1 had just had her eighth birthday.

With the sporadic approaching din, Mia set aside her work in dismay. She could hear the commotion of Jake and her own three young children as they clattered down the long tunnel that adjoined the Cotton Room.

With the return of her noisy throng, she'd have to finish the remaining journal entries later.

• • •

Marie smiled as she sauntered through the door of the new clinic. It had taken them many years of planning and construction but finally the modest new medical center was complete. The group had debated and vacillated for months about the optimal location for the facility, nearly everyone had crusaded for the clinic to be situated near *their* particular homes. Finally an unusual alliance of Ynez and Osman rallied the others for the construction of the infirmary in the lone remaining vacant warehouse halfway between the Hawaiian Beach and Southwest Desert

Habitats.

Marie idly ambled around the cozy office. It was more spacious than the tiny open shelter that she shared with Floyd, which for far too many years had often doubled as the group's health center. At last she would have a much-needed separation between her personal life with Floyd and her professional life as the local doctor.

She sat on the new swivel chair that Nick had recently delivered and contemplated the impending examinations. The invariably pregnant Mia and her oldest youngster were due shortly: Mia for a prenatal exam and three-year-old Annie for a persistent middle ear infection. Osman had cracked a molar several days earlier and promised to stop by for a consultation on his way to the desert habitat to deliver some provisions.

But Marie was particularly anticipating a checkup scheduled for the early afternoon. Xea had turned eight-years-old just two days ago. Her imaginative and independent niece had arranged for an office visit on her own a week earlier. Marie had called Ynez to verify the appointment and the woman had lamented that her precocious daughter now spent most of her time alone far off in the unoccupied Cityscape tending to the little dogs and exploring the elaborate buildings.

The doctor vowed to discuss the growing estrangement between mother and daughter with the youngster during the check up.

• • •

Marie nibbled at the delightful lunch that Osman had left on her worktable after his examination. She noted her observations about the stout man's dental problems in her journal. Marie's eyes narrowed as she wrote, she would need to investigate how to cap the man's damaged molar. The doctor winced, she also required some sort of antibiotics for poor little Annie's endless ear infections. Perhaps if she could find her way around in the convoluted Library of All Human Knowledge, she could instruct the Minion Robots to manufacture the appropriate remedies.

Pleasantly jingling bells announced a visitor at the front door. "Come on in," Marie beckoned.

The door clattered open and the petite black haired girl meandered into the room with the huge gray tabby cat. A tremendous smile flashed across Xea's face, "Hi Aunt Marie."

The woman rose from her chair to greet the gregarious eight-year-old. "Hello, sweet pea. I'm impressed by your unusual diligence regarding your health. Have you eaten yet?"

The girl nodded absently as she fiddled with the profusion of mysterious medical instruments that she'd discovered neatly laid out on a white cloth next to the examination bed. "What's this gizmo?" She pointed to a curved, symmetrical implement composed of an assortment of tubes.

Marie smiled at the girl's inquisitiveness, "That's called a stethoscope, it's for listening to the heart." She led her curious patient to the examination bed. "Climb up and sit on the edge."

The immense feline poked tepidly around the office for several minutes before curling up under the worktable for an afternoon nap.

Xea ascended the two steps and hoisted herself up onto the high platform, finally sitting edgy and erect. "This isn't going to hurt, is it?"

Marie laughed, "Have you ever had a painful checkup, Xea?"

The diminutive girl pressed a finger to her cheek and tilted her head in contemplation, "Um; no."

"Why do you think this one will be any different?"

"Well;" a grin darted across the youngster's face, "I found some stuff in the Library about checkups." She bit her lip and gazed off for several seconds as she recalled her recent discovery. "Doctors stick patients with pointy metal thingies sometimes and the kids always cry afterwards." Her eyebrows arched up accusingly.

"Pointy things?" Marie wondered out loud, "Do you mean injections or vaccinations?"

Xea nodded.

"No worries, my little pixie." Marie retrieved a small flat stick from the table of instruments, "There are no diseases in our world that would require anyone to be vaccinated." She held the tongue depressor expectantly in front of the girl's mouth, "Besides, your Uncle Floyd and I haven't gotten around to fabricating any hypodermic needles yet. Open please." The doctor studied Xea's mouth. "You have *such* nice teeth."

"So no poky things?"

"Nope; not today." Marie checked the patient's eyes and ears before she pressed her fingertips along the girl's jaw. The doctor selected the recently discussed stethoscope from the table. "I'll put this part in my ears and hold this against your chest."

Xea flinched when the cold instrument touched her skin.

"Have you had any unusual problems or pains, sweetheart?" Marie slid the bell of the stethoscope across the girl's chest."

"No," Xea said with a look of discomfort.

"How's everything at home?"

"Good," the girl replied evasively.

"You're not having any problems with your parents or Tin?" Marie probed.

"That *stupid* brother of mine!" Xea's face suddenly flashed with indignation.

Marie set aside the stethoscope and studied her now angry niece. She would need to be calm and impartial if she hoped to draw out the especially perceptive girl. "Mmm; tell me about the difficulties with Tin."

"It's not fair!" Xea pouted melodramatically, "Tin gets all of the attention at home. My mom thinks he *so* perfect because he's quiet and studies all of the time." She snickered, "He can barely contact the Master/Minion and he has *no* idea how to get to the Library of All Human Knowledge."

"Well;" Marie tipped her head empathetically towards Xea, "only you, Uncle Floyd and I are really equipped to interact with the Master/Minion."

"What about Kat?" the girl reminded her Aunt.

The dozing feline looked up at the mention of its name.

"OK, and Kat. But even Mia, who should have no problem, struggles with it. You've always been very talented at contacting the M/M." She tousled the girl's hair, "Climb down and you can try out some new equipment for me." The doctor directed the still-fuming young patient to an odd teetering contraption that took up most of the floor space against one wall. "Step up on this platform, please."

Xea wobbled precariously on the strange contraption. "What are we doing now?"

"Your daddy built this for me, it's a balance scale," Marie snickered, "and not a very attractive one, I'm afraid." When the undulations of the oversized apparatus diminished, the doctor added counterweights to the opposite platform. "How *is* your dad?" When Marie judged that the two sides were in balance, she tallied the weight, "Twenty kilograms." She jotted the results in her journal.

"He's pretty good, but I hardly ever see him." The youngster sprang from the device, which caused the counterweight laden opposite end to crash to the floor.

"Alright; back up against the wall," the doctor directed the girl. "Straighten up, please. Why don't you see your dad very much?" Marie made a mark on the wall just above Xea's head. "A hundred and nineteen centimeters. You are *such* a wee lass."

"Daddy's always working on projects somewhere," the girl lamented. "He's *so* busy all of the time."

"I'm afraid that your Uncle Floyd is the same way." The doctor grinned, "I just figured out where to find this information. Would you like to know how big you'll be as an adult?"

Xea nodded.

Marie closed her eyes and read through the growth chart that she had summoned from the Master/Minion. When the doctor had retrieved the desired information, she blinked several times to force her eyes to focus on her patiently waiting niece. "Most likely about forty-eight kilos and one hundred and fifty-four centimeters by age eighteen."

"I don't know what that means," Xea shook her head.

"OK;" Marie struggled to find a more tangible reference for the child. She held her hand across her chest just below the armpit. "This tall, which is a bit shorter than your mom. Just about the same size as Sabina, I think, although you'll probably be a bit thinner."

Xea sighed heavily.

"That's a good size for an adult," Marie assured the girl.

"No; it's not the size." The youngster's shoulders slumped,

"I just *really* miss Sabina."

Marie slipped her arms around the suddenly downcast child, "You talk to her using the robots, right?"

"Sure; but when I explore some interesting part of the Cityscape and I find something that's really weird, I just wish that she could be there to tell me about it."

The doctor sifted through the clues for several seconds before she spoke, "You're lonely, aren't you?"

Xea nodded gloomily.

"According to your Uncle Floyd, Sabina's not likely to return for years." Marie endeavored to find some encouraging news for her despondent niece. "You can always talk to me about anything that concerns you."

The girl considered the offer carefully. "Alright," she finally answered.

Marie checked the girl's pulse, blood pressure and temperature before she declared her to be in good health. "How's Kat been doing? Since you've been tending to matters in the Cityscape, the jungle kitten hardly ever visits with me anymore," the doctor said as she updated the medical records.

Xea's face brighten at the mention of the beloved cat, "I'll tell you a secret. But you *can't* tell anyone, not even Uncle Floyd!"

"I promise," Marie summoned her most solemn face.

"Kat will do things for me."

"Nothing involving the Minion Robots, I hope, since you're not allowed to command them," she reminded the little girl.

"NO!" Xea replied remorsefully, "Nothing with robots. Kat goes places and checks on things for me. Don't get mad, but sometimes Kat brings me things."

"What things?"

"My dad gave Tin that blanket that I had when I was little, but he didn't even ask me first. I really wanted it back but he said I was too big for baby stuff."

Marie set aside the paperwork, "Then what happened?"

A self-satisfied smirk darted across the girl's face, "Kat snuck into our house one night and carried the blanket back to the Cityscape. He was sleeping on it the next day when I stopped by to feed the dogs."

"Kat's quite a friend," Marie mused. Apparently, her niece was having the tabby carry out her dirty work. She glanced at her earlier notes, "Xea can you help me with something?"

"Sure."

Perhaps she could use this little exercise to further bond with the girl, Marie thought. "Can you help me find some things in the Library of All Human Knowledge?"

"I could do that," Xea intoned, "but I will need to see your eyes."

Marie swiveled around in the chair to face the youngster. The monstrous feline flexed under the worktable before standing to witness the proceedings.

Xea pressed her small hands against Marie's temples, "Make a picture in your mind about what you want...."

"A picture of me fixing Osman's tooth?" the doctor faltered.

"No; the Master/Minion won't know what you want, just imagine his broken tooth."

Marie nodded slightly, "OK; I see a bunch of information about what teeth are made of, how the crack crosses the molar, those sorts of things. Now what?"

"Think about what it should look like when it's fixed."

The doctor frowned, "The Master/Minion's just telling me about the mended molar."

"Aunt Marie, push the picture of the broken tooth into the picture of the repaired one."

The woman manipulated the imaginary dental work. "OH! Now I see it."

Marie watched ghostly images of Osman's damaged tooth quickly repair itself with the application of a quick-setting liquid plastic of some sort.

Over the next several hours, the intrepid little girl guided the physician through dozens of overlapping medical vignettes in the vast Library of All Human Knowledge.

Kat voiced an odd yowl that drew the preoccupied woman and child back to the small infirmary.

Marie slumped with fatigue, "Thank you, Xea." The woman rubbed her aching forehead, "I think that it would have taken me weeks to find this on my own."

The youngster beamed at the praise of her unusual talents.

"Now I'll need to get the robots to fabricate the remedies for Osman and Annie," the doctor lamented. She scrawled several notes, "Is there anything else that we need to talk about before we both head home, young lady?"

"Yeah; I think so," Xea nodded apprehensively. "Sometimes I hear the voice of a lost boy. His name is Gunther and is all alone." Xea's body tightened in torment, "He's *really* scared."

"Normally I'd be worried about a patient hearing mysterious voices." After the exhausting quest through the daunting library, Marie dearly wanted to return home to the tranquil Beach Habitat. "Your Uncle and I think that sometimes the Master/Minion leaks dreams into our heads. Perhaps the same thing is happening to you." She stood and retrieved her medical bag from the wall peg. "I don't think that you need to worry about a lost boy." The doctor pulled open the door of the clinic and the cat darted across the feebly lit warehouse to the tunnel entrance. The girl and the woman walked together towards the aperture door and the long passageway beyond. "Are you heading home, sweet heart?"

They stepped through the slit and the girl watched the feline bolt off. "No. I need to feed the dogs," Xea sprinted down the dim tunnel after the big tabby.

"Let me know if you hear any more voices," Marie called halfheartedly to the rapidly receding child.

• • •

The two tiny dogs noisily devoured their food on the ornate front porch of the Castillo del Nocturno house in the Cityscape.

Xea shook her head in mock disgust as she watched the messy display, "You guys are little piggies!"

Nudge finished up the last of the morsels in his bowl and eyed the tidbits that remained in the other dog's bowl. The scrappy black dog pushed aside the more submissive brown one to gulp down the sparse remnants. The dogs waddled around on the porch before they ventured down the steps to the deserted Victorian-lined street.

For several minutes Xea contemplated the dogs as they frolicked before she pushed open the heavy door of the mansion. She was in no hurry to return home to the sweltering heat and her unappreciative family.

She ambled aimless around in the huge house.

Xea ascended the long stairway to the third story. She wandered across the huge landing to a tidy guest bedroom. She loved this particular room, it was larger and less cluttered than the cramped cottage that her family shared. A barely perceivable breeze caused the lacy window curtains to quiver about the open sill. Xea leisurely fingered the intricate objects laid out on an elegant dressing table.

114

She gently opened an ornate jewelry box and idly examined the charms and bracelets that it contained. Her hand caressed an embellished hairbrush and a now inoperative windup desk clock.

The girl meandered across the room and joined the big cat curled up on a huge white pillow on the bed. The purring animal's head tilted back and she scratched the beast's chin. "I wish that I could stay here all the time with you."

"Xea..."

The cat's head popped up; its yellow eyes grew disquietingly large.

"Xea...are you there?" the ethereal voice called to the girl.

It was the lost boy, Xea realized. *"Are you OK, Gunther?"* she thought.

"I've been cast out and now I'm all alone," from far off the downcast voice resonated though her mind.

The cat and the girl stared at each other in alarm.

Xea's black eyes narrowed, *"What can I do, Gunther?"*

"Come...help me..." he stammered.

"I..," she struggled to find a way to aid her despondent friend, *"I can't, they won't let me use the robots to find you."*

Kat tapped insistently at her arm as she shivered from the frightening encounter.

"*I need help. I'm stuck here and I'm so lonely,*" the boy pleaded.

Kat batted at the girl and she stared into the feline's eyes. For a tense minute, they contemplated the seemingly intractable problem.

Xea sighed with relief, "OK." She nodded and Kat bound off of the bed and trotted away.

"*Gunther; help is coming but it's going to take awhile.*"

• • •

"Mama; Kat's here!" Annie called from the Cotton Room.

Mia's head popped through the aperture door from their living quarters at the sound of the child's voice. "That's strange, Kat hasn't stopped by for years."

"It just leapt through the door from the tunnel," the girl reported. She wrapped her arms around the big animal but the feline was in no mood to play just now. The beast struggled away from the child and padded to the soft gray mound that dominated most of the room. A piercing howl reverberated around the chamber as the striped animal pawed insistently at the fibrous mass. Minutes passed before the cat turned and trotted back to the exit, the required deed now done.

"That was *really* weird," Mia remarked to the little girl.

• • •

The High Priest clasped his palms together in blessing as he turned to his acolyte, "I see that the Sacred Silk is creating another creature to dwell amongst us."

"Yes your holiness." The robed young man bowed to the exalted leader, "It is small. I believe that the Silk will soon favor us with an animal."

"Whatever the revered Silk produces is sacred, my son," the priest declared.

As it had done many times before in the dim sanctum of the Cult of the Silk, the gray filaments slowly gathered together to form a new cocoon.

11. Elation

Marie squeezed the little red ball that had sat forlorn for so long on the brown table in the back of the beach hut. She had seen the trivial plaything several times a day for over five years; the familiarity of the object had caused it to slowly blend into the vague surrounding clutter of the shelter.

She wistfully recalled tossing the jaunty toy about as a rare shred of merriment during the tedious misery of her dozen year exile.

Marie lobbed the lopsided sphere from hand to hand; "Floyd."

He looked up from the task of sorting through the sack of supplies that he had gathered the previous day.

"When we do finally assimilate other people into our group," she snatched the ball from the air with her right hand, "*where* are they going to live?"

"Well;" Floyd briefly considered the few surplus areas of their Realm, "I don't know."

Marie set the ball back down on the table, "Could we expand into an adjoining Realm?"

"I guess we could," the engineer stroked his chin, "but I think that the mysterious neighbors on the anti-spinward side would probably put up a fight and on the spinward side is the ruins of Kurt's old area."

"I realize that," she nodded, "could the Minion Robots tidy up the destruction and restore Realm 18?"

She could tell by his far-off gaze that he had already begun to plan a grand remodeling project for the shattered region.

"Mmm; that's a good idea, Doctor Mayfield," Floyd finally acknowledged.

• • •

While he donned his space suit for the morning trek, Old Floyd felt almost guilty as he admired the sparse campsite that he'd assembled. He was rapturously alone, far-off in the still and quiet caverns. As much as he loved his little family in the crowded desert shack, he had always been a much more solitary person. The incessant din and demands of his housemates tended to muddle his thoughts and hamper his ability to solve especially nettlesome problems.

Although the idea of setting up a temporary outpost at the barrier door was originally suggested by Nick, Old Floyd had enthusiastically championed the idea. The proximity to the Outer Causeway would allow him to more easily investigate the long tunnel network without the added burden of returning home between each expedition.

If he was ever to successfully explore the surface and hopefully locate the coveted 30 Gigahertz Array, he'd have to spend as much time as possible on the endeavor.

The engineer clamped his helmet into place and the air reprocessor switched on. He activated the air lock and started off for a distant and promising door that he had discovered opposite the entrance to Realm 15.

• • •

She'd had only the most basic instruction in dental surgery as a Med student, Marie mused as she peered into Osman's gaping mouth. The rotund man lay still but obviously uncomfortable on the examination bed in the clinic.

The Minion Robots had concocted a viscous white jelly for the man's damaged molar along with the weird little patch of sticky orange material that Marie had applied to Annie's arm which had swiftly cured the girl's ear infection.

The doctor mentally reviewed the impending procedure.

She hesitantly dabbed the jelly on the cracked tooth. The odd substance promptly thinned on contact with the enamel and spread swiftly across the crown to fill the void. In seconds, the tooth was mended. Marie admired the now flawless molar. Apparently dentistry in the thirtieth century was finally quick and painless.

"All done," she smiled at the big man.

Osman clamped his mouth shut and jutted his jaw out several times to appraise the rapid repair work. He sat up on the bed and grinned, "You are now my new favorite dentist, Doctor Marie."

She fondly studied the effervescent fifty-four-year-old black man; he was universally adored by all of the members of the group. Osman had a surprisingly clear understanding of the idiosyncrasies and tribulations of the various residents. Unlike herself, Marie realized, he had lived through many lifetimes with each of them.

120

"Could you help me with another patient, Osman?" Marie asked timidly.

His eyes grew absurdly large at the unexpected request, "I can't stand the sight of blood."

She laughed, "It's nothing like that, I'd like your advice about Ynez and her dreadful fits of depression."

A dark and doleful look of concern appeared at the mention of the despondent woman, "The poor thing often gets glum when she has difficulties with her house mates. Many times in the past, I've helped her out of a funk when she struggled with some misdeed of Floyd or Nick."

Osman stared intensely at Marie, "But this is much worse. I think it has something to do with the two pregnancies and the little rug rats constantly under foot."

"That was the essence of my diagnoses, as well."

The man's toothy smile returned, "I recall that my father fought off the occasional blues with an preposterously overpowering cup of espresso made with the beans from one of his many Kenyan plantations." Osman chuckled, "After a tiny cup of the dark sludge, the gloom was gone but he couldn't sleep for days."

She sighed; "I think that it would take years of painstaking effort to produce a good cup of coffee."

"Why don't you have the robots produce some antidepressants?"

"I considered that," she vacillated, "I didn't do particularly well in the Psychology rotation as an intern and the brain is a delicate and complex organ. I'm likely to create more problems than I solve using medications."

"Mmm, could you produce some sort of happy thoughts in Ynez's head?" he asked jokingly.

The doctor held her fingertip to her forehead, "Strangely, that might work." She contemplated a possible therapy, "I wonder if I could use the Master/Minion to induce a sense of mild euphoria?"

She poked at her old friend's generous belly; "I'd need to try this out on a willing volunteer first."

"I don't know," he sighed in mock apprehension, "experiencing intense happiness without having to visit a street vendor in a sleazy neighborhood, that doesn't sound possible."

They laughed together.

"Yeah; I'll do it."

Marie pressed her hands on either side of the man's skull and stared into his eyes, "We'll start out with mild euphoria. I don't want to inadvertently blow your head off of your shoulders."

"Thank you for that," he giggled.

The woman directed the Master/Minion to induce a state of mild euphoria in Osman for one minute.

All signs of tension drained out of the man. A contented

look of pleasure settled over Osman as if he'd been wrapped in a warm and cozy blanket after enjoying a fine meal with cherished friends.

"This is *really* nice," he cooed. An immense grin of satisfaction stretched across his face.

The minute elapsed and the smile slowly faded.

"Better than the finest pharmaceuticals and libations," he assured her.

It had worked stunningly well, Marie realized, perhaps too well. "Besides elation, how did you feel?" she probed.

"Warm and happy without a care in the world."

The doctor considered the consequences of a permanent state of blissful apathy, "If you had an important and trying task to accomplish, would you endeavor to do it?"

"No," he suddenly realized the folly of overpowering pleasure.

"If I left you in that state for long," the doctor warned, "you would jubilantly starve to death in a pile of your own filth, I'm afraid. Do you see what I mean? Brain chemistry is remarkably sensitive to slight changes."

"I think that this *could* help Ynez," the man ventured, "but at a much more subdued level."

Marie concocted a second experiment for her volunteer. She quickly excused herself and retrieved a prop that she hid discreetly in a pocket of her blue frock. The woman clasped the man's head and commanded the Master/Minion to produce only a state of slight euphoria in the man.

His demeanor brightened immediately. He had the cheerful look of a child anticipating a bedtime story.

Marie tossed the concealed red ball to the joyful man. "JUGGLE NOW!" she bellowed.

Osman merrily complied with the unexpected requirement and flawlessly flung the orb from hand to hand with quick showman-like flourishes. The experiment ended and he held the ball high in beaming victory.

"I think we may have stumbled upon something," the doctor wryly noted.

• • •

After eight long hours in the space suit, Old Floyd floated giddily at the final barrier door. During the protracted trip, he had gradually become more excited by the progressively weakening pull of gravity. Two hours earlier, he'd discovered that headlong leaps forward were a much better means of propulsion down the narrow passage than the scuffling trot that he'd employed elsewhere.

Now he peered eagerly through the small square window centered on the thick door. In the distance was the ebony blackness of space adorned with droves of unwavering stars. For at least fifteen millennia, not a single one of the nearly two hundred humans aboard the Cerces had seen the celestial vastness that stretched out before him.
He cautiously opened the door.

The effects of the sudden infinite openness of space were both thrilling and nauseating. Old Floyd clung steadfastly to the doorjamb. To his left, the far-off curve of the horizon brightened in anticipation of an imminent sunrise. The nearly featureless gray surface glinted in the stark intensifying light.

Silhouetted by the approaching dawn, he could see several distant blocky structures. A curious collection of many large white spheres adored with strange protuberances were arranged in orderly rows near the horizon.

Old Floyd studied the odd and mysterious relics for many minutes.

The immense glowing corona of the sun rose above the horizon.

Scorching white light spilled across the surface. He clinched his momentarily sightless eyes shut against the dazzling onslaught. An unusual warbling trilled in his ears. Old Floyd turned away from the sunrise and blinked hard several times to overcome the blindness. The maddening sound intensified to a loud drone.

He tipped his head down to study the environment displays below his chin just inside the dome of the helmet. *LETHAL COSMIC RAY LEVELS* blinked ominously on the small screen.

The old engineer reluctantly pulled himself back into the safety of the tunnel and closed the massive protective barrier. Further investigation of the fascinating surface would have to be careful planned to coincide with nightfall, he grudging concluded.

• • •

Floyd grasped the sides of the Minion Robot as he spoke to the distant woman, "So everything is going well in Realm 3, Sabina?"

"Other than the infestation of giant pink orangutans, everything is fine," she teased.

The man was momentarily confused by the humorous retort, "Very funny. How's Jasper working out?"

"In the boudoir or elsewhere?" she salaciously asked.

"Uh; elsewhere."

Sabina chortled at his prudishness, "Marie was right about his unwavering diligence. Jasper has zealously worked for years almost exclusively on the Threesia castle. It's really quite a spectacle now."

"How are you doing with your supplies?" he wondered.

"I could use more of that blue fabric that you have in great gobs. The robots are rather tardy at replenishing the small amount that is stored here," the woman complained, "but no momentous problems."

"I hate to keep bringing this up," Floyd pestered, "but I'd like to introduce some other unfamiliar clones into your Realm."

"Now is not a good time," she evaded.

Floyd frowned at the abrupt brush-off, "Sabina, we've really got to get this repopulation effort moving forward. I'd like to add a Jessica or Ben clone to your group in the near future."

A long silence followed.

"I'll think about it," the woman dismissively replied.

• • •

"I'm not sure what it was that I saw," Old Floyd confided to his attentive daughter. "There were many of those huge strangely shaped objects way off near the horizon of the Cerces."

Xea nodded to her father as she contemplated his intriguing description of the first exploration of the surface. From the warm flagstones of the patio, the ubiquitous gray cat seemed to follow the man's tale along with the girl.

"Even though I was stuck at the doorway, I could tell that the machines must have been really important at sometime in the past."

The girl had an all-consuming interest in his exploit that might prove useful, Old Floyd realized. "Do you have any ideas about those weird things, sweetie?"

She wriggled her nose and pouted as she considered the conundrum. After several seconds, Xea drooped in defeat, "Dad, I need a better description if I'm going to find what you want in the Library. Big round machines with pointy thingies won't work."

"I don't know how else to describe them."

"Can you draw a picture?" she coaxed.

The man ambled into the house and returned with a fat pencil and a sheet of paper. He set about doodling a scratchy rendition of the stunning vista that he had encountered earlier.

Xea carefully studied the rough sketch as her father worked. "What's that?" she pointed at a series of wiggly lines that protruded from a misshapen circle.

He carefully drew a splayed fork that extended from a second nearby circle.

"That looks like the arms on a Minion Robot," Xea commented.

The man reflected on the depiction and his memory of the unusual structures, "They were very similar."

"OH!" the girl exclaimed, "I found something!" She pointed to the side of one of the circles, "Was this part white with some small black gizmos?"

"Yes, and a few dark lines radiating out like this," he scribbled an asterisk on the side of the object.

"OK Dad, I've got it," she declared. "They're called '*Lawo giztak mignom*,' which means, '*servant construction spacecraft.*' They are some of the giant robots that built the Cerces," Xea explained to the astonished man.

12. The Silkies

Kat pawed at the girl's arm.

Xea set aside the journal that Aunt Marie had loaned her and stared for several seconds at the insistent animal, "You're right; it's time."

She stroked the huge cat's head, "I hope that it goes well."

The cat twisted away from the girl and paced uneasily across the worktable.

• • •

In the dark sanctum, the young acolyte stopped his tedious task and studied the motionless animal that the Sacred Silk had produced. The sleeping creature had gray fur adorned with rippled black stripes. He pulled aside a large piece of the hallowed threads to reveal a velvety serpent-like tail tucked between dainty paws equipped with sharp sickle-shaped claws. The robed novice pried back the last of the delicate cocoon.

It was a cat. No doubt an agent of the underworld, he assumed. He was obligated to immediately inform the High Priest of this dreadful omen.

The young man apprehensively considered the wisdom of leaving the devil's emissary unattended as he sought out the Holy Leader. The sleeping cat *seemed* to pose no imminent threat.

After many minutes of careful consideration, the acolyte crept silently away to seek out the blessed old leader.

The huge yellow eyes of Feline Test Subject: Gray Tabby 215.900 opened just as the naive man departed. The cat stretched its long legs and arched its supple back. The feline stood and carefully appraised the surroundings. An urgent mental dictate required that the animal must quickly flee and locate a lost human male. The task was prescribed by another of its kind allied with a young human female.

The muscular animal bound to the floor of the dim chamber and padded to the door. The ever-moving ears twitched, two men were approaching the room. Immediate escape was not possible. The cat crouched in wait amongst the shadowy recesses.

The acolyte meekly spread the flaps of the door for High Priest and followed the revered one into the sanctum.

The old man crowed at his good luck, a cat would be a fine sacrificial offering. His malleable flock of simpleminded fools would be easily cowed by the spectacle of the demonic animal's ritualistic death as atonement for their supposed sins.

The acolyte stood motionless; the frightful animal had vanished.

"I was only away for a hare's breath, my master," the frightened young man bowed subserviently. "Perhaps the Evil One has reclaimed his agent."

The old man smiled sardonically, "I am assured that the divine spirit of the Silk would prevent the demon's escape. Cast about the sanctuary, my devotee, and you shall find the beast."

The young man searched for the missing animal.

When both humans faced away from the exit, the concealed cat sprang from the room.

The swiftly departing feline startled the men.

"Capture the monster!" the Priest bellowed.

Gray Tabby 215.900 easily escaped from the humans.

• • •

In the lightless void of the caverns in Realm 19, Gunther extended his hand, "I've been expecting you, my fellow."

The soft and warm body of the sizable animal glided smoothly under his palm.

"I know that it's very dark in these caves, so you surely can't see me," he squatted down to allow the creature to brush against his face.

The animal purred loudly.

"Xea mentioned that you would make a friendly sound." His fingers gauged the size of the unfamiliar creature, "I have never known a cat. You are much larger than I expected."

The feline circled affectionately around his legs and mewed softly several times.

"I suppose you haven't eaten since your escape from the Priest," his hands searched around for the small cache of supplies. "Three days ago I could see through your eyes when the two humbugs tried to find you in the sanctum," Gunther located a meager bag of food and retrieved some morsels to offer to the cat, "I was quite amazed."

The animal fastidiously sniffed at the handout.

"I hope that you like it. Someone brings it to here while I sleep. I suspect that it is a robot because the gullible Silkies are terrified of the dark."

The cat nibbled at the food.

"My savior Xea has an animal like you. She calls her friend Kat." The food had vanished from his hand and the pleasant purring had resumed. "I believe that I will call you Katoo."

He hoisted the heavy creature and carefully sat on his bedroll, "You are so very soft and warm." Gunther nuzzled his new companion; "I was cast out by the dimwitted Silkies when they were goaded by the craggy old Priest."

The contented sound of the cat prompted him to continue his story.

"They have always been afraid of me because I wasn't begat like everyone else by their stupid Silk." His sudden laughter caused the dozing animal to stir, "I came out of a woman's body! Xea says that long ago all humans were produced in that way."

"When I was very young, the Priest convincing the Silkies that I was a dangerous monstrosity. Even my mother would not care for me. But I could call the robots," he chuckled.

"The machines fed me and protected me from the tireless torment of the Cult."

"Gunther? Is that you?"

"Xea! My friend has found me!" He gently stroked the now sleeping cat. *"I have named it Katoo."*

"That's amusing. It's a pun," the girl replied.

"I don't fathom..."

Xea giggled as much at his simple nature as the unwittingly cleaver word play. *"It's the second clone, so it's number two and it's sequence number is 900 which has two 'Os' at the end like the name: Katoo."*

"Oh; I understand," he finally acknowledged as he caressed the slumbering feline in the cool blackness of the cavern.

• • •

Except for brief excursions to satisfy urgent bodily functions, Katoo had stayed close to Gunther for more than six months. The ever-vigilant cat had confirmed that a lone Minion Robot occasionally delivered supplies when the human slept.

Xea realized that it would be a big step and certainly a major act of defiance for Gunther to finally leave the sanctuary of the caverns as she coaxed him along from her distance vantage point in the Cityscape.

"You can do it. Katoo remembers the way."

There would certainly be difficulties when the twosome encountered the members of the Cult of the Silk.

It was still far too dark for her to see though his eyes or those of the animal. The reluctant creature had allowed Gunther to hold onto the tip of its tail for guidance. The strange partnership of human and cat inched along in the blackness. She was eager for the two shuffling travelers to reach the tunnel where the big cat would instruct the Master/Minion to activate the overhead lights and allow her to finally glimpse Gunther.

"Katoo has stopped, Xea. We are at the portal."

Xea could now see through Katoo's eyes as the big animal leapt through the aperture door and glared at the ceiling light panels, which caused them to switched on. Gunther pushed his sack of belongings through the slit before he struggled clumsily past the tight opening. He stood upright and Xea studied her reclusive friend.

He was a man, she reluctantly noticed, not a boy, as she had always assumed.

To her dismay, she could not see anything through his eyes. Gunther continued to fumble about as if he was still in the dark.

Perhaps he was blind, she frowned.

"Gunther; are you sightless?"

"Yes;" he admitted, *"my vision disappeared soon after I was released from my mother's body."*

He had an odd way of speaking, Xea realized. *"When did you leave her body?"*

"Long, long ago." He grasped at Katoo's tail but the creature struggled away, apparently now unwilling to continue the previous traveling arrangements.

"Xea; my companion will no loner guide me. What shall I do?"

For several minutes Xea interacted with both of them as she considered the wishes of the animal and the needs of the blind man. *"Katoo has agreed to guide you if you carry it."*

"My arms will truly grow tired."

A knowing little smile crept to Xea's face, *"I will tell you how to make a knapsack for Katoo. Then you can carry your friend on your back."*

"Very well."

She instructed the blind man as to how to fabricate a cat carrier with the spare supplies on hand, all the while watching his fumbling efforts through the animal's eyes. At last she was satisfied with his work. He hoisted the knapsack with the animal in place onto his back. Katoo squirmed around and explored the tight pouch for nearly a minute before drooping its front legs over the man's shoulders.

"Can you see what Katoo sees, Gunther?"

"Yes...but I will need enlightenment to know of what it means."

"Katoo and I will help you," she assured him.

For many hours Gunther struggled his way down the long passageway.

"How did you end up in the caverns?" Xea asked the man as he traveled.

"The acolyte tricked me into following him by telling me that a better place awaited me." Gunther somberly added, *"When he knew that I could not escape, he said the Priest wanted me dead. Then he left me alone. I called out to you soon after he withdrew."*

"That's terrible!" Xea frowned.

"Yes," he replied.

The big cat hissed in alarm and Gunther stopped.

"Someone is about." His open hand slid appraisingly over the tunnel wall, *"I know this place. This is the edge of the Silkie encampment."*

Xea could see far down the passage, *"There's a doorway nearby, where does it go?"*

"I smell the water of the Ritual Pool, surely that is what you see. Each of the Silkies must survive a plunge into the bottomless waters by the Priest to prove their devotion to the Cult."

A frightened old woman appeared and shouted at the travelers, "Gunther, you demon child, how did you return from the underworld?"

He turned towards the voice, "Mother; I came back from the forbidding caves to live with the Cult."

The crone recoiled at the sight of the gray feline draped over her son's shoulder, "The High Priest will be enraged that you were abetted by the devil's emissary."

Xea was unnerved by the vehement woman, *"Katoo and I may not be able to guard over you alone, Gunther. Will you summons a Minion Robot for more protection?"*

Katoo yowled in concurrence.

The woman fled in fear from the man and the large feline.

"I am seeking a robot," Gunther acknowledged.

Within minutes, the old Priest and half a dozen followers set upon the blind man laden with the anxious cat.

The ancient robed man held his arms high in contempt; "You were cast out of the Cult for your abnormalities. You and your familiar must *not* taint the Sacred Spirit of the Silk."

Gunther growled menacingly at the mob, "You stupid fools! I have strong friends now. Your precious silk merely does the bidding of the powerful Master/Minion!"

"Blasphemy!" the High Priest shouted. "KILL THE PROFANE INTRUDERS!"

Xea watched in horror as the mob led by the acolyte advanced ominously towards the sightless man.

The hands of the fervent mob shoved and scratched at the pair. Katoo savagely bite the palm of one of the frenzied assailants.

A bizarre crackling sound wavered through the passageway. Someone shrieked.

The acolyte stiffened and fell backward. The arcing projections of a robot sent several Silkies into convulsions. The remaining followers regrouped around the High Priest for assurance.

The blind man, the big cat and the surly robot stood their ground.

"I will NOT be cast out again!" Gunther warned the believers.

Xea cheered the man's astounding deliverance.

The High Priest watched in dismay as the young acolyte twitched spasmodically on the ground. For now the old man's trickery and bluster were useless, but in the future he certainly would strive to inflict a wicked retribution upon the devil child.

"This is the work of the Evil One!" the Holy man luridly declared to his terrified followers.

13. Personae non gratae

Old Floyd sprang forward across the shadowy gray surface of the Cerces. In the three years since he first gazed at the hostile terrain, the tireless engineer had developed many improvements that had allowed a more meticulous inspection of the area that surrounded the barrier door. His space suit was now equipped with a darkened faceplate to protect his eyes from the omnipresent glare along with a particularly sensitive new radiation detector to monitor any outbursts of cosmic rays. But his favorite innovation was called 'the kangaroo jump and thrust down.'

In the nearly weightless environment of the surface, he faced the real possibility of leaping completely off the colossal spacecraft; carried away to a perpetual low orbit by his upward momentum and the feeble gravitational tug of the Cerces.

The sixty-five-year-old astronaut judged that his stupendous jump had carried him sufficiently far afield. He pulled on the twin cords that ran down the front of the space suit which opened the spring-loaded valves of the upward facing gas spheres strapped to his back. Two short bursts of compressed air forced him gradually back to the surface. He adjusted the trajectory of the slow descent with tiny additional pulses of air from each of the tanks.

He gently touched the surface and squatted down to begin another vault forward.

Although both Marie and Floyd had accompanied him to the surface intermittently in the past, neither had enjoyed the giddy excitement of bounding headlong into space.

Old Floyd flexed his legs and propelled himself upward again. Far off near the horizon, the mysterious flat structures and the long forsaken construction robots remained well beyond his reach. The engineer's goal today was a modest square structure that protruded from the landscape an hour or so from the barrier door.

The continuous bobbing reminded him of an odd carnival ride that he had ridden with his older cousins at the county fair in Socorro, New Mexico. He realized that both Xea and Tin would have relished the annual event.

Right now his brilliant and spunky eleven-year-old daughter was most likely in the clinic with Marie studying the complex endeavor of medicine as the most recent of her many interests. His stoic and studious eight-year-old son would certainly be tending to his studies in the Southwest Desert school with the gaggle of Mia and Jake's four boisterous children. Ynez would be haphazardly teaching the youngsters.

The old engineer sighed, things had gone terribly wrong with his mate. The woman's wild mood swings had caused Xea to grow impatient with her volatile and unpredictable mother. The girl regularly avoided her academic work with the others, preferring instead to find her own enlightenment in the serene and alluring Library Of All Human Knowledge or by the side of the ever-pleasant and accommodating Doctor Marie.

Xea frequently spent her days exploring the Cityscape with the big gray cat, she would return home after protracted absences to endure her mother's torrid rage or teary embraces. The girl was often at odds with her even-tempered brother as well, taking the boy to task for the preference that Ynez seemed to show him.

Old Floyd's ruminations about his dysfunctional family were interrupted by the looming structure. He pulsed the down thrusters to settle on the top of the low edifice and carefully climbed down the side of the building.

A long unused barrier door dominated one side of the small structure. He tapped on the dusty face of the portal but it did not respond to the prompt. The engineer shone a light through the small window and examined the gloomy interior. It was merely an empty shell of a building.

Old Floyd speculated that the odd building might have been sealed off during the construction of the robotic research ship by the Master/Minion to satisfy the strict prohibition against cross contamination by marauding or merely curious humans from Earth or the space colonies.

After a short rest, he reluctantly set off for the barrier door that led back to the Outer Causeway. The old engineer casually wondered if Tin would join him on the surface someday. The boy would likely fit into Sabina's small space suit that was still stowed in the caverns of Realm 3.

Old Floyd glanced at the small clock that was attached to his sleeve, he had just two hours and four minutes before the sun would rise over the horizon and bombarded the surface with gamma rays and high-energy subatomic particles.

• • •

She was doing it again, Xea noticed.

Her mother stood taciturn and transfixed on the sweltering flagstones staring far-off into the desert while the group of bewildered students waited for further instruction. The girl would have to mention to Aunt Marie that her mother's steady dose of euphoria required additional adjustments.

"Aunt Ynez?" Seven-year-old Annie eventually appealed to the befuddled teacher, "What should I do next?"

The woman blinked several times before she focused again on the uneasy students.

"If you've finished your penmanship practice, Annie; I'd like you to begin the report about your family."

Xea watched her mother shuffle around the worktable to inspect the scrawly work of Annie's three little siblings before she scrutinized the achievements her own progeny.

Ynez stopped to hover over Tin and spent a protracted period adoring the neatly inscribed quadratic equations that her son had produced.

"Very good Tin!" Ynez raved to the boy; "You are my *most* perfect scholar today."

Xea rolled her eyes in contempt, her mother had praised her brother perhaps just a bit *too* vigorously.

The woman held Tin's work up for everyone to see, "This is the well-ordered effort that I expect from all of you."

Ynez tussled Tin's hair and returned the worksheet to the boy. The teacher ambled over to Xea and inspected the girl's morning accomplishments.

Xea had painstakingly drawn a human liver and carefully labeled the many obscure parts in both English and rEn sprak.

"No." Ynez shook her head in disdain, "This is unacceptable, young lady."

Xea frowned at her implacable mother.

"I asked you to write a skit in the Shakespearean style, not doodle your time away with silly artwork.

Xea's face hardened into a mask of seething rage. She would no longer endure the turbulent idiosyncrasies of her mother. Xea snatched the drawing from the table and stormed out of the Southwest Desert Habitat.

The nascent young woman tromped alone down the dreary passage bound for the Cityscape. As angry tears trickled down her hot red cheeks, Xea vowed to never again return to her stifling birthplace.

• • •

"Hello my dear," Marie kissed Floyd on the cheek as he entered the clinic.

"I see your protégé is helping out again today," the man commented.

Xea absently waved to her uncle from the kettle of steamy water as she tended to the task of sterilizing a set of surgical tools for the doctor.

Marie smiled to her esteemed mate, "What brings you to the Sawbones' lair, Mr. Bernal?"

He slumped onto the swivel chair, "I talked to Sabina and she finally agreed to add another clone to Realm 3."

Marie noticed her niece eavesdropping at the mention of Sabina. "I guess she yearns for more of an audience than Jasper can prove," the woman chuckled.

"Perhaps," Floyd said. "I managed to browbeat her into allowing us to decide who will be cloned into the group next."

Marie thought for several minutes. "Flossey is unacceptable; she and Sabina would eventually have a gruesome battle to the death, I'm afraid." The doctor tapped her finger to her cheek several times, "Ben might work out, but I'm not sure how he and Jasper would get along."

Xea folded a steaming towel over the now sanitary instruments that she had arranged on a metal tray and joined the adults.

"I think that it will have to be Jessica," Marie asserted. "After all of the dreams that I've had about her, I'm a bit worried that the poor thing will be terribly frightened about emerging from a cocoon surrounded by unfamiliar people."

"I suppose that's true," Floyd nodded.

"Aunt Marie," Xea interjected, "I think that you can tell the Master/Minion to produce *any* version of a Jessica clone.

Maybe a Jessica 2 or 3 wouldn't be as scared as a Jessica version 1 clone."

The woman smiled at her petite assistant, "That's a good idea, squirt."

"How did you figure that out?" Floyd wondered.

Xea nervously considered how to answer the question; she had Kat carefully specify which version of the gray tabby should be produced for Gunther, but might her aunt and uncle frown upon her de facto dictate to the Master/Minion?

The girl shrugged nonchalantly, "Something that I remember from the Library, I guess."

Marie closed her eyes as she often did when she interacted with the Master/Minion. "We can choose any of the four versions of Jessica. I've only interacted with Jessica 2.8 and Jessica 4.37. Four point three seven was the final one to be produced, she was killed in Kurt's star-crossed war with the robots," the doctor noted.

"A Jessica 3 or 4 would remember you from the exile in the caverns but not from your much later confrontations with Kurt," Floyd reminded the woman. He smiled as he noticed that both Xea and Marie shared the same look of intense concentration.

"Alright then;" the woman finally answered, "Jessica four point something it is."

• • •

Gunther sat glumly with Katoo. Even though he had forced his way back into the Silkie encampment years ago, the cult members had never included him in any of the group's undertakings.

The loyal animal was his only tangible companion and often his sole protector. The vigilant cat had thwarted many sneak attacks by the acolyte and the other followers by quickly summoning a robot to stand guard at the earliest signs of trouble. But the harassment had continued unabated.

The High Priest had commanded that no one should supply food or water to Gunther or Katoo. As had occurred during his banishment, a robot would often deliver supplies to him when the Silkies slept.

Gunther's lone diversion besides the big cat was his frequent exchanges with Xea. He eagerly followed his now twelve-year-old friend's many deeds and disasters. He had suffered along with her when she made the momentous decision to forsake her family and live unimpeded in the Cityscape. Gunther had vicariously studied the complexities of the medical profession through the young woman's experiences. He often assisted Xea by locating particularly obscure information in the Library or directing the Minion Robots to surreptitiously investigate an unusual aspect of her own homeland.

But his own situation was untenable and they both knew it. Eventually the Silkies would stumble upon some way to destroy him.

Xea was incensed by the unending misdeeds and insults that he regularly endured. His friend had vowed to somehow relieve his suffering. But Xea's nearly insurmountable obstacles to helping him were the great distance that separated them and her inability to directly command the Master/Minion and the robots.

For now at least, they would each have to tolerate their own difficulties and dilemmas alone.

• • •

Playing cards and poker chips were scattered everywhere.

"Grown men," Marie shook her head in dismay, "I can't believe that you two were fighting. Not so many years ago, you had patched up your long running animosities."

She studied Jake's black eye and swollen lip. "What was cause of these shenanigans?"

The man flinched as the doctor pressed her fingers probingly around his inflamed eye socket.

Nick dabbed at his bloody nose as he sat on the bench at the massive table outside of the cottage in the Rocky Mountain Camp.

Osman and Old Floyd warily watched over the two bruised combatants to assure that no further skirmishes would erupt.

"Well?" Marie pressed the men for an explanation.

Neither Jake nor Nick was willing to describe the disagreement to the doctor.

Osman sighed heavily and finally recounted the events that led to the fistfight. "We were playing five card draw, as we often do on Thursday nights." He stared at Nick with displeasure, "And this nitwit kept bringing up his carnal exploits with the various woman of our group."

Nick pressed his hand to his brow in shame.

"He decided to tell us all about his torrid misbehavior with Mia before Jake returned to the flock," Osman scowled at his longtime chum. "He even claimed that he fathered Mia's first-born. *That* was when the punches flew."

Marie cringed at the report by the big man. She and Floyd had long feared that Nick's dalliances with Mia would cause rifts in the small band.

Floyd joined the impromptu inquisition with a very distressed Mia. Marie told the two about the altercation between the men.

The elfin woman sobbed as she fell to her knees in front of Jake, "I am *so* sorry. I never meant to hurt you!"

Touchingly, Marie noticed that Jake's hands quivered as he stroked the repentant woman's chestnut hair.

Jake looked pleadingly up to Marie and she nodded in acquiescence. The slim and scraggily man led his tearful mate away to discuss the unsavory revelations.

With the departure of the disgraced pair, Floyd stood next to Marie to consider what penalty should befall the perpetrator of the misdeeds.

"Nick why did you do those things?" Floyd asked in exasperation.

"I don't know," he replied. "In all of our many years here, I've nearly always had a sweetheart or lover." The man's blood stained face showed a hint of contempt, "After I

emerged, all of my past girlfriends had found other mates. But I was most galled by Mia's infatuation with that moron Jake."

Marie fumed at the man's sexual manipulation, "So it was all a twisted effort to injure Jake?"

Nick nodded slowly, "I guess that it was."

The doctor scowled at his reply.

Marie, Floyd and Osman traveled to the nearby workshop to debate as to what should be done with the rogue while Old Floyd stayed behind watched over Nick.

After several hours of agonizing deliberations, the jury returned with a remedy.

Marie spoke for the group, "In light of the history of my homeland and my own dreadful experiences with Kurt's Tribe, this particular penalty seems rather ironic to me. But so be it."

After he had appeared to be surprisingly unrepentant for most of the last several hours, Nick looked suddenly very remorseful.

"Shortly;" the woman announced, "you will exiled to Threesia until Sabina decides that you may return."

14. Impediments

News of Nick's forced departure spread quickly. Nearly everyone agreed that the talented craftsman would be missed for his abilities to fabricate innumerable household items, but most realized that the robots could now quickly produce these objects in his absence.

Osman was particularly dismayed that his thousand-year friend would no longer be close at hand. The big man was well aware of Nick's lecherous misbehavior and the detrimental consequences that they might bring, but was still deeply saddened that the seemingly eternal camaraderie of the two men was now ending.

The four woman of the group uniformly felt that the lascivious man had violated the sense of discretion that such a small society required and deserved the exile that would be imposed upon him.

• • •

"Here it is," Old Floyd pointed to the markings that his younger clone had inscribed on the wall of the Outer Causeway eight years earlier. The aged engineer had long desired to travel to Realm 3 and had quickly volunteered to escort Nick to the far-off region when the unexpected opportunity presented itself.

"Out of the two of us," Nick wearily noted, "I'm the luckier one."

Old Floyd opened the barrier door that led to the caverns of Realm 3, "How do you figure that?"

Nick grinned irreverently, "I'm more than happy to stay here with my dear old friend Sabina and I won't have to repeat that damned trip through the Causeway anytime soon."

The old engineer winced at the prospect of the return trip in several days time.

The men trudged down the long tunnel and entered the airlock. After many minutes spent waiting for the equalization of pressures, the barrier door opened to the dark caverns.

Old Floyd hoisted the helmet off of his head and scrutinized the shadowy area in exasperation, "Where is she?"

Nick held up a light disc and slowly scanned the forbidding terrain; "Sabina was suppose to meet us here, right?"

"Yes. I talked to her just before we left." Old Floyd was well aware of the considerable difficulty that the men faced if they were forced to find their own way through the unfamiliar area.

After many minutes, they set off without the promised local guide.

Hours later, the bleary twosome located the eerily quiet Cotton Room of Realm 3. The men cautiously pushed their way though the aperture door and entered the faintly lit chamber.

Two bowls of food and the woman's dark cloak laid unattended on a low bench near a developing cocoon that was suspended high in the mass of soft gray fibers.

"Something's gone wrong," Nick noted.

Old Floyd directed a bright beam around the room, "Sabina apparently abandoned everything unexpectedly."

The flaps of the door to the bedchamber rustled menacingly.

Both men recoiled as a sinister black shape emerged from the doorway.

The arcing tines of an ebony robot swept threateningly around the small room.

A deep twangy voice reverberated from beyond the ominous machine, "Sebastian, STOP!"

The dark Minion complied.

A sturdy copper-haired man embellished with bristly red sideburns stepped from behind the stationary robot.

"Welcome gentleman, I'm Jasper," the big Australian extended his hand to the frightened visitors. "Don't mind the mechanical help," he rapped his knuckles on the apparatus, "he can be a bit scary on his first greeting." The man added with a smile, "He's really just a big puppy dog barking at strangers."

Old Floyd obligingly shook the man's hand, "Where's Sabina?"

Jasper's smile faded, "I'm afraid that the Empress of

Threesia is inconsolable right now." He led the travelers into the gloomy bedchamber.

Sabina was propped up in the middle of a huge white bed. She waved dolefully to the three men.

Old Floyd studied the downhearted woman for several seconds. "Why didn't you meet us in the caverns?" he asked.

The petite woman wiped her bloodshot eyes. "I talked to Floyd after you left," she trembled with pent-up emotion, "Old Mia just died."

• • •

While Marie waited for the others at the big table in the Rocky Mountain Camp, she contemplated the remains of her elderly friend. After the doctor had performed a cursory autopsy, she and Xea had painstakingly dressed the old woman for the memorial service. Her young assistant had become especially uneasy during the somber preparations, no doubt grasping for the first time the finality that all deaths demonstrate.

Floyd and Osman had gently carried the body from the cabin to the plank table. Osman was quite devastated by the loss of both of his closest friends on the same day. Marie resolved to watch over the man for any signs of depression in the coming weeks.

The day before, he had called her in the clinic on the ancient telephone, reporting in a panic that Old Mia was writhing in pain on the floor of the cabin. The doctor had sprinted to the distant habitat but the old woman was dead when she arrived. The autopsy had revealed that most of the woman's blood had drained into her chest cavity from a breached artery. It was called a 'ruptured aortic aneurism' she grimly remembered from medical school. There was nearly nothing that would have saved her dear friend.

That wasn't true, Marie realized.

Had she detected the distended blood vessel months or even years ago, difficult but plausible remedies *could* have prevented the untimely death. As the physician for the small group she was duty-bound to uncover any concealed maladies and promptly treat them.

Beginning tomorrow morning she would carefully evaluate the health of each of the members of the group and work diligently to treat any underlying problems.

Floyd arrived and squeezed her hand in condolence, "How are you feeling, Dr. Mayfield?"

"Sad," she replied. Marie realized that she had not witnessed a memorial since joining the group. "What do we do with her body after the funeral?" she whispered to Floyd.

"Nothing. We leave it here. In a day, it will be gone."

"Gone?" the woman asked in surprise.

"Yeah, I'm certain that the Minion Robots carry off the remains, but in thousands of years, no one has ever seen it happen," Floyd noted.

"What do they do with bodies?" Marie wondered.

"I don't know," he shrugged.

• • •

A day after Old Mia's sorrowful farewell both Marie and Floyd had resolutely taken up some of the various projects that had been long left half-done.

The doctor carefully checked the man for any signs of hidden disease. Thankfully, Floyd's health was excellent.

The engineer spent most of the afternoon in Kurt's old Realm where he inspected the derelict restoration project that he had started many years earlier. Fortunately the robots had repaired the gaping wall rupture and the Master/Minion had reestablished a musty but breathable atmosphere. Much work remained to be done before humans could once again safely dwell in the devastated environment.

Together Floyd and Marie carefully considered all of the available information about the diverse groups in the other Realms of the Cerces for the first time. Although three regions had achieved favorable marks in the Hyperion Index, nearly all of the other groups showed mediocre or dismal societal evolution. Marie concluded that they would eventually have to visit each Realm and evaluate the locals personally. Floyd concurred with the woman's sound reasoning.

• • •

"Good luck," Sabina glumly told Old Floyd as they stood together at the barrier door in the caverns of Realm 3. She kissed him on the cheek to emphasize the sentiment. Even after two days, he noted, she still looked particularly miserable about Old Mia's death. The engineer hoisted the space suit helmet; "I should be back to Threesia in about twelve hours."

She nodded to the man and, trailed by the ever-present Sebastian, started her slow journey back to the Cotton Room bedchamber.

Old Floyd checked over the spare second robot that Sabina had loaned to him. The machine would accompany him on the excursion to a surface tunnel located four hours away in the Outer Causeway. Xea had recently learned of the passageway and the elderly astronaut was eager to investigate the surface on this side of the Cerces.

Sabina had convinced him to take along the spare robot, suggesting that perhaps he could ride the machine piggyback around on the surface. As amusing as that activity sounded, he merely wanted to investigate the robot's potential for future work in the harsh environment of space.

He led the obedient machine through the airlock and eventually on to the Outer Causeway.

Hours later, the robot stalled partway down the surface tunnel. Old Floyd nudged the malfunctioning machine in the narrow confines of the passage but to no avail. The robot deactivated and partially blocked the tunnel. He struggled for many minutes to dislodge the broken Minion.

Old Floyd continued on to the surface without his defective partner. The engineer theorized that the robot was perhaps too far from its unknown power source or that the Gravity Amplifying Substance that allowed the machine to hover effortlessly was ineffective in the near weightlessness of the surface tunnel.

At the robust surface door Old Floyd quickly discovered that the long journey had been worthwhile. Some distance away he spotted an orderly collection of dozens of dish-shaped antennas that bore a striking similarity to the Very Large Array Radio Telescope on the Plains of San Agustin near his grandmother's home in New Mexico. The huge installation might well be the 30 Gigahertz Array that Xea had told him about many years earlier.

Near the horizon, the man noticed several deep craters and the shattered wreckage of what seemed to be a large spaceship. Sadly he would be unable to investigate the intriguing finds today, he had left the essential but very bulky down thruster backpack at the cavern campsite in his own Realm.

After nearly an hour of studying the vista from the safety of the surface door, the old man reluctantly returned to the Empire of Threesia without the malfunctioning robot.

• • •

Marie sat at her worktable in the clinic with the thick volume of her nearly full journal opened in front of her. She had scribed each of the names of the thirteen group members at the top of more than a dozen pages. The doctor was determined to closely monitor the health of the throng.

"Alright Xea, I have a new task for you."

The twelve-year-old set aside the stethoscope that she had been using on the dozing gray cat.

"Since you are more aware than anyone of your mom's strange mental state, I'd like you to hunt around in the Library for anything that might describe her disorder."

Xea's face rippled with concentration, "OK; I'll see what I can find."

Marie returned to the journal entry about Floyd. She felt oddly annoyed that she'd discovered nothing more serious in her now nearly forty-year-old mate than a slightly twisted left toe and several tiny intestinal polyps. Perhaps she hadn't looked close enough to find any obscure maladies or maybe, she skeptically concluded, he really *was* in good health.

"Aunt Marie?" Xea interrupted the doctor's ruminations.

"What is it, peewee?"

"You need to give me Tier One Access so that I can enter the Human Psychology section of the Library," Xea mentioned.

The woman tipped her head in confusion, "I don't have Tier One Access myself, how can I bestow that particular privilege upon you, my dear?"

The young researcher stared at the doctor, "I'm *sure* that you can, I figured this out a long time ago. You and Uncle

Floyd reign over the Cerces and the Master/Minion. You can give Tier One Access to anyone but yourselves."

"So I can let you or Uncle Floyd muck about in Level One?" Marie slowly repeated.

Xea nodded, "And he can do the same for you."

The woman considered the peculiarities of the ship's security system. "That must keep people from poking around willy-nilly on their own, although I can't imagine why Psychology would be off limits," she smiled. "OK; you should have permission now. Please be careful."

"Thanks!" the girl smiled.

The two worked silently on their tasks for several hours.

"Oh my gosh!" Xea suddenly exclaimed.

Marie set her pencil aside.

"This has *got* to be it," the young assistant grinned triumphantly.

"Did you find something that might help your mother?"

"I don't know if it will help," a fleeting look of revelation darted across her face, "but I'm pretty sure that she has something called Terminal Clone Syndrome."

"Really? What's that?"

Xea pressed her hand to her forehead as she recited the newly discovered information, "In 2287, a cloning researcher named Quan Ziegfeld discovered that many clones had achieved the delusion of immortality after repeated duplications of their memories and bodies. This misconception was often shattered with grave psychological upheaval in the final individual if the clone line was terminated unexpectedly because of disease or other reasons."

Marie frowned, "I guess that the Master/Minion's strange prohibition against cloning everyone who has become a parent essentially terminates the Ynez line."

"Well;" the girl interjected, "I'm not *really* convinced that parents couldn't be recloned, Aunt Marie. But that's way off topic."

The diminutive detective continued, "It says that symptoms in individuals affected with Terminal Clone Syndrome include severe depression, trancelike states, unrealistic expectations of others and extreme mood swings."

"I'm afraid that sounds just like your mom," the doctor noted. "How am I going to remedy that condition?"

"I don't know," Xea replied.

While her aunt considered how to treat the unbalanced woman, Xea used her new access privileges to surreptitiously investigate another more sinister section of the immense Library of All Human Knowledge intriguingly entitled 'Human Test Subject Dossiers.'

15. Rescue

"I don't know what to do," Xea confessed to the stationary robot as she sat on the front steps of the grand home.

"Well;" from far away in Threesia, Sabina answered, "it *does* sound like your little friend Gunther is in a sticky predicament with those zealots."

"I've got to try to get him out of this mess," the twelve-year-old pouted.

The woman laughed unexpectedly. "This is *not* something that can be accomplished by one, my dear fledgling."

"What do you mean?"

"You will need powerful allies," the clever woman reported. "I didn't build that splendid Cityscape by myself. Nick made most of the furnishings and doodads for me, now he's doing the same in Threesia. Your daddy figured out how to construct the buildings. Osman and Mia did much of the mindless fiddly work. I just came up with the ideas and tried to stay out of the way."

Xea considered the profusion of intricate dwellings in the Victorian-lined habitat that she had always assumed were the sole creation of her aunt.

"OK;" the aspiring rescuer sighed, "I'll talk to Aunt Marie about Gunther's problems."

• • •

After many weeks of preparation, the elaborate plan was well underway.

Xea had been surprised that both Uncle Floyd and Aunt Marie had been willing to venture to the Cult of the Silk to liberate Gunther and Katoo from the vengeful Silkies. She restlessly waited in the ornate attic bedroom of the Castillo del Nocturno house for her uncle to return from the Outer Causeway after he completed the first part of the bold scheme. She knew that Gunther had prepared carefully for his escape and would be waiting when the rescuers arrived.

● ● ●

In the remote and dark caverns of Realm 19, Marie deposited the many sections of her space suit in the huge sack. She would not need the bulky garment for the daring and dangerous return with the blind man and the large cat. Floyd waited uncomfortably in his own space suit at the airlock door for the woman to finish packing.

She handed him the overstuffed bag, "I feel surprisingly nervous right now."

"Be careful," Floyd warned her. "It will take me two days to travel to the rendezvous point."

"For most of that time, I'll be hiding out here in lavish splendor," Marie giggled as she surveyed the rocky surroundings.

She wrapped her arms around the bulky waist of his suit and kissed him, "You did remember to instruct the Master/Minion to intercede if any problems develop?"

Floyd smiled nervously, "Ah; I will. The robots will stun, not kill; so you'll have to run like hell."

She poked him lightheartedly in the midsection; "I will see you in two days, Mr. Bernal."

He lumbered off with the unneeded equipment.

Marie dined on a light meal and slept soundly after the long journey. She spent most of the next day cautiously traversing the hazardous void of the caverns. Though Gunther had reported to Xea that the Silkies rarely entered the frightening rocky labyrinth, the blind man *did* warn that the old Priest and his acolyte sometimes undertook secret rituals there. Marie spent her second night well concealed within sight of the aperture door that led out of the caverns.

She drifted in and out of restless sleep. Marie's past experiences with the malevolent members of Kurt's Tribe had brought a keen edge to this endeavor, but she was also especially curious to learn more about this fanatical group. As she waited out the hours before her quick dash to liberate Gunther, the woman reviewed what was known about the Silkie society.

Using her new Tier One access, she noted that the Master/ Minion had rated the Cult of the Silk as a paltry 334 on the Hyperion Index. Not the lowest marks on the Cerces, but a dreadfully poor performance compared to Bashiir's group with the high marks of 754. The Silkies had apparently done little to advance their society from the Stone Age level where all of the Realms had started out. The Cult was currently ruled by a tyrannical leader who did not tolerate unpopular ideas. The group's mistreatment of weak members was particularly glaring as was witnessed by the endless persecution of Gunther.

Marie gasped as she uncovered an ominous new notion that the Master/Minion had affixed to the Hyperion information about the Silkies: *This group of Human Test Subjects is currently under watch for termination due to poor performance.*

Would the cyber overlord of the ship abruptly murder misbehaving humans?

She quickly scrutinized the Hyperion file for Kurt's Tribe. A horrific directive blinked in red: *Human Test Subjects terminated due to inferior performance and environmental destruction.*

Marie surmised that the attack on the robots and the ensuring damage to the Realm had pushed the group below the arbitrary limit of 250 points set by the Master/Minion. As she had long suspected after her vivid nightmares of the Robot War, the few remaining survivors had been summarily executed when the Master/Minion had swiftly evacuated the air from the Realm.

Sabina had been right all along; for thousands of years they had been nothing more than mere test animals to be promptly discarded when an experiment went awry.

Marie realized that she and Floyd would need to alter the Master/Minion's unquestioned edicts regarding the ruthless slaughter of humans.

She switched on a tiny light disc and examined Floyd's prized pocket watch that dangled around her neck. It was time to venture down the hallway to the Silkie encampment.

Marie warily poked her head through the aperture door. Without her familiar light disc pendant, the tunnel remained disconcertingly unlit. The darkness would both conceal and hinder her. She slid her hands slowly over the smooth walls of the passageway as she advanced.

With Xea's help, Gunther had estimated that it would take three hours for Marie to traverse the distance from the caverns to the edge of the encampment.

Hopefully Floyd and the others would be ready.

• • •

The engineer had whittled the required equipment down several times but the burdensome supplies were near the limit of what the two people could safely carry.

Xea and Kat had loitered a bit too much in the vast tunnel network that honeycombed the Cerces beneath the various Realms, Floyd groused. With luck, the threesome would not be late for the surprise rendezvous. His niece had never been through the complex passageways and many airlocks that had ultimately led to Floyd and Marie's serendipitous discovery of the Master/Minion.

"Be ready," Floyd warned the dawdling travelers when they at last reached the proper airlock, "your ears will pop after the door closes." He activated the unit. An alarm sounded and the pressure swiftly rose.

The cat pawed madly at its ears. Xea winced in pain. Floyd coughed and swallowed hard several times.

The alarm stopped and the air pressure stabilized.

Floyd tapped on the floor of the tiny room and a small round door slid open to a dim and watery world.

• • •

Her heart was pounding.

Marie stood motionless in the dark tunnel at the entrance to the Silkie encampment. She could hear the faithful as they chanted the morning prayers. Gunther would expect her during the chaos that typically followed the daily ritual. She could hear the old Priest's lamentations about the sins of the flock.

In a moment it would be time to start.

• • •

"...and so may the Sacred Spirit of the Almighty Silk absolve the unworthy of their sins," the High Priest extolled.

"Amen," the flock murmured in unison.

"Be mindful today of the Spirit that created us, my children," the old man sternly admonished the worshipers. He clapped his hands twice and the group dissipated.

The acolyte helped the High Priest down from the pulpit. "That was quite inspiring," the young man fawned.

"Meek modesty is a virtue, my son," the Priest reminded his pupil.

"Of course, Master," the acolyte bowed subserviently.

The young man frowned when he glimpsed the tall and unfamiliar person resolutely striding around the shadowy parameter of the encampment. "Your Holiness, I suspect that a wicked omen has befallen us." The acolyte pointed to the willowy woman who was helping the blind man to his feet. The big cat paced nervously about the legs of the two.

The Priest sneered contemptuously and bellowed, "Who is this deplorable marauder that desecrates the hallowed Cult of the Silk?" The indignant old man marched towards the interloper.

Marie spun around to face the cantankerous leader and his subordinate. Her eyes narrowed.

The Priest and the acolyte stopped a few paces from Marie. The Silkies quickly gathered behind their leader to cut off the escape route.

They were trapped!

The old man growled, "I sense the Evil One is amongst us."

Gunther clung anxiously to a strap that dangled from the woman's waist.

Marie defiantly thrust her arms towards the mob, "I have come for the blind man and the cat."

The Holy man quickly engaged the opportunity to provoke bloodshed, "I will not permit the devil child and his demon animal to escape to the underworld."

The Silkies advanced menacingly. The followers' hands grabbed and flailed at the captives.

Marie balled up her fist and struck the younger man squarely in the jaw. The stunned assistant tumbled backward, which momentarily distracted the rabble. She shoved the old man aside.

Katoo dashed off.

Two Minion Robots appeared and forced the Silkies away from Gunther and Marie.

One foolhardy fanatic leapt forward and a robot sentinel laid the man out with a crackling flash of high voltage.

They must escape!

"Hold on to me, Gunther!" Marie shouted to her frightened ward.

The old Priest seethed at the nearly lost opportunity. He lunged at the mysterious woman intent on blocking the getaway. The man fell short and tumbled to the ground.

Marie's head jerked unexpectedly at the Holy man's sneak attack. She quickly recovered and trotted off towards the aperture door with Gunther.

The robots prodded the horde of Silkies into a tight cluster and held them while Gunther and Marie hurried down the tunnel.

They would have less than five minutes to vanish undetected.

The woman jumped through the nearby portal and wrestled her blind companion through the door. Katoo bound in behind them.

"What are we doing?" Gunther panted in panic.

Marie quickly surveyed the shadowy and unfamiliar room.

There!

The surface of the Ritual Pool wavered. Floyd's head popped up and he swam briskly to the edge.

"Trust me Gunther and we will escape!" the woman barked.

She sat him down on the low wall that surrounded the pool and swiftly stripped him of his clothes. Marie tossed the unneeded garments into the pool. "You're going into the water!"

The horrid rants of the old Priest and the frenzied chants of the Silkie mob echoed down the passageway.

They were coming!

Floyd flung the bulky canister onto the walkway and quickly gathered the blind man's clothes.

Marie gripped Gunther's trembling shoulders. "Don't panic," she whispered hoarsely. With a shove, she propelled him backwards into the choppy waters.

Floyd grabbed the man just before his head went under. "Put this in your mouth and breathe normally." He thrust the scuba mouthpiece in place. "Everything is going to hurt like hell for a minute!" Floyd sucked on his own air supply and dragged the frightened man under the frothy liquid.

Marie turned in panic. The sizzling crack of the Minion protectors was just outside the door. She pried open the canister and forced the big cat into it. The animal howled in terror. She slammed the carrier shut and heaved the heavy chamber into the roiling water. The watertight carrier bobbed wildly in the waves.

The woman stopped in alarm. Something was missing! Marie clutched at her neck. The pocket watch was gone!

The terrible shriek of an electrocuted Silkie filled the air.

Marie glanced quickly around the walkway for the missing keepsake.

Nothing!

She sprang into the Ritual Pool, snapped the canister's tether to her waist strap and sucked in a gigantic breath. Just before her face went under, she flicked open the ballast valve and the carrier plunged down, dragging the woman with it.

Her ears squealed as she rocketed downward into the dark abyss. Marie looked up at the rapidly receding surface. Through the silvery undulating liquid far above she could see the followers as they searched about for the escapees. She dare not let even the tiniest bubbles free to disclose their whereabouts.

The canister hit the bottom with a dull thud and the spent woman bobbed limply from the tether. In the crazy delirium of growing asphyxia, she felt hands pry open her mouth. She bit weakly on the hard rubber of the mouthpiece. Cold air filled her lungs.

It was Floyd. He unsnapped the canister and tugged her sideways to the huge inlet pipe. As her senses returned, Marie watched the man swim up into the dimly lit opening with the cat-laden cylinder. He returned and nudged her through the intake.

Marie broke the surface and stared at the odd assembly that had awaited her appearance.

One rather damp and unhappy gray cat stood next to its dry twin. A nearly naked and very befuddled blind man had his hands pressed tightly to the face of her petite and beaming niece. Floyd popped up beside her in the tiny opening with a huge grin. The woman pulled the mouthpiece out and kissed her mate in triumph.

"WE DID IT!"

• • •

The Priest cringed as the acolyte dabbed at his wounds. The dreadful robots had relented and left the bruised and battered flock some time ago, but the sting of the infidels' escape pained him more than his abrasions. The old man considered how to explain the disturbing incident to his uneasy followers.

The Holy man grinned cynically.

He would cast the lithe and mysterious woman as the very embodiment of the wily devil. Surely the dull fools would accept that interpretation. The Priest opened his hand and examined the trinket that he had snatched from the tall intruder.

The ornate pocket watch ticked resolutely in the dim sanctum of the Cult of the Silk.

16. Triumph

The return trip through the lower tunnel network was jubilant and unhurried. Gunther expressed his thanks many times to the group for their colossal effort on his behalf. The four people gleefully recounted their personal recollections of the encounter with the Silkies and the triumphant rescue. The twin cats engaged in a comical chase game that involved dashing madly through the many side passages.

The merry group stopped along the way and spent nearly an hour at the unusual chamber of the Master/Minion. Both Xea and Gunther carefully investigated every surface of the matte black room. For many minutes the blind man lay upon the wide vertical black cylinder that dominated the center of the chamber. After much prompting, the two young people reluctantly left the physical embodiment of the otherworldly intelligence that they both knew so well.

Marie grinned as she watched Xea gently lead the blind man along by the hand. The woman prodded Floyd, "Where is our new member going to live?"

"I hadn't even thought about that." He pointed to the pint-sized shepherd and her charge, "Let's ask them."

Marie stopped the slow procession, "Have we decided where Gunther will live?"

Xea giggled at the query.

Gunther nodded. "I'm going to live with Xea in the...Cityscape. Is that what it's called?" he turned to his companion.

174

"Yes," she rolled her eyes at his confusion about the name of the fantastic habitat.

Marie's brow arched up, "Some members of our group might consider that arrangement to be improper."

"Why?" the young man wondered.

"Long ago on Earth," she started, "unrelated young adults of the opposite gender didn't live together without first getting married." Marie stopped to consider the many reasonable exceptions to the convention, "At least that was the expectation in most societies."

"What about Grandma Camille?" Xea asked. "My dad said that she lived with several different men and didn't marry any of them."

"You're right," Floyd nodded.

"Does it matter that we're not on Earth?" Gunther mentioned. "I would be *very* sad if Xea was separated from me."

"Me too," the young woman kissed him on the cheek.

"It's not so much the living together that I'm worried about," the doctor said.

Xea laughed at her aunt's innuendo, "Are you afraid that I'll get pregnant?"

"I hope that you will eventually, sweet pea," Marie shifted uneasily at her niece's candidness, "perhaps after your eighteenth birthday."

"That won't be a problem," Xea stated. "If we ever get around to lovemaking," the teen smiled, "which I don't think will be anytime soon, I've have already prepared for it by adjusting my ovaries. I'm temporarily infertile."

The doctor was astonished, "How did you manage to do that?"

"It was quite common on Earth after 2100," Xea said matter-of-factly. "I studied the process for awhile and told Gunther about it. He had the Master/Minion instruct the neural interface in my brain to produce the right amount of different hormones." She shrugged, "So now I can't possibly get pregnant."

Marie marveled at the exceptional young woman's resourcefulness, she had essentially altered her own body to manufacture a never-ending built-in contraceptive.

• • •

"This is a little bedroom," Xea led the blind man into the small room off of the third floor landing at the Castillo del Nocturno house.

He tugged unexpectedly on her hand.

The young woman stopped the tour, "What is it, Gunther?"

The man wearily rubbed his unseeing eyes, "I don't know what a bedroom is, Xea."

She smiled at his childish and curious nature. Since Uncle Floyd and Aunt Marie had left them many hours ago, he had used his ever-moving fingers to carefully study the many different rooms and innumerable small objects in the huge house. The slow trip through the well-appointed kitchen had taken nearly two hours. She had patiently explained the purpose of dozens of gizmos and gadgets that Sabina had amassed over the centuries.

"A bedroom is a comfortable place to sleep."

Gunther nodded at her short description.

Xea guided him to the slender side table against one wall.

"Oh; I hear something!" he exclaimed.

She set his hand on the elegant desk clock that diligently ticked away the time.

He caressed the smooth old timepiece, "It has a wonderful sound. I suppose that it helps people to sleep."

She smiled, "It probably does but clocks are meant to keep track of time."

"Time?"

"When things will happen in the future or how long ago something occurred in the past, that's what time is."

When his fingers glided along the smooth tabletop, she took his hand and escorted him to the lovely bed with fluffy white blankets and several generous pillows. "This is where you can sleep."

Gunther contemplated the soft mattress and fine bed sheets. "I am very tired," he mentioned.

"Climb onto it and lay down."

He curled up on the blankets and quickly drifted off.

Xea sat on the edge of the bed in slowly waning light of early evening and carefully studied the handsome and inquisitive man that she had known from afar for so long.

She had found a worthy partner.

• • •

It was a lovely night in the Southwest Desert, Old Floyd thought as he reclined on the easy chair. A cool breeze wafted across the still warm flagstones. The guiro-like percussion of crickets reminded him of the Latin American music that he had often heard in New Mexico as a boy. Thousands of stars glinted in pastel shades of blue, yellow or amber in the sable sky. The faraway mesas were mere black silhouettes that protruded into the fervent celestial spattering of incandescent specks.

He knew the stunning nocturnal spectacle well; it was part of him. The primal desert vista was simply mimicry that dozens of past Floyds had toiled to perfect. It was an idealized forgery of an arid land on a far-off planet that he had committed to memory long ago.

Ynez joined him on the patio.

He took her dainty hand and beckoned her to share the easy chair with him.

She curled up next to him, "It's so nice to have you home."

Old Floyd winced at the implied misconduct. He had been primarily engaged in the arduous and drawn-out effort to further the fortunes of the entire group. But he had grown to regret his neglect of his kin and the beloved desert homestead. Although he could never admit it to his mate, he *most* missed the easy companionship of his effervescent daughter.

In the lulling and tranquil night on the starlit patio, Ynez softly stroked his cheek.

"They're back from the rescue," he mentioned.

"I know," she whispered in resignation.

He kissed the top of her head; "I met Gunther this morning, he's very nice."

Ynez nodded.

"He's staying in one of the Cityscape houses with Xea and her menagerie of animals."

"Osman told me," she sat up and stared at him with a look of pallid misery.

"What is it, dear?" he could see that she was struggling to maintain a sense of calm.

"I'm disturbed that our twelve-year-old daughter is living with a much older man."

Old Floyd considered the conundrum for many minutes.

Everything that his independent and worldly first born did

was infused with careful consideration and flawless reasoning. No doubt she had sensibly explored every conceivable variable before she decided to host the blind man in the Cityscape.

"I think that we will just have to accept that she is wise beyond her years and leave it at that," he was certain that Ynez would not be happy with his declaration. Old Floyd wrapped his arm around the troubled woman. "My grandmother told me that long ago her Spanish ancestors often married off their daughters at age twelve."

She reclined next to him again on the easy chair, "Why on Earth would they do that?"

Old Floyd smirked, "Grandma Camille thought that more than a little bit of it had to do with getting temperamental teenagers away from their frazzled parents. But the custom had many practical aspects. A frighteningly high number of all woman died in childbirth before the 1900s, the sooner they began the process, the more likely that a few heirs would be produced before the mother's untimely death."

Ynez shook her head in dismay, "I'm pretty sure that Japanese girls waited until they were eighteen or so to settle down with a man."

"Catholicism was the big difference between Japan and the Spanish world," he sighed. "Sexually attractive young woman are highly desirable to men everywhere, but an unwed mother and her illegitimate child is an unpardonable sin in the Roman Catholic Church."

She listened carefully to the story delivered in his soothing baritone voice.

180

"Properly marrying off your preteen daughter under the watchful eyes of the local clergy insured that the bridegroom and his family would ever after defend and vouch for the parentage and legitimacy of the offspring."

He laughed, "Apparently young Spanish mothers were thought to be too overburdened with child rearing and too fearful of divine retribution to veer off the path of respectability."

Old Floyd studied the sweeping multitude of imitation stars, "Like it or not, older men living with young women is nothing new."

"So you're OK with our daughter's male room mate?"

"Yes," he nuzzled Ynez's long black hair. "If anyone can handle that situation, Xea can."

17. The fortuitous partnership

It had come to her in a flash, Marie realized.

She had been bobbing about on the surfboard in mediocre waves as she waited around for something much better. The combination of the gentle movement, the warm midday glare and the white noise steadiness of the surf had set her mind to wandering. She recognized it now, many months later, as a most fortunate episode of rambling free association.

Now as she sat in the place of honor with Floyd, patiently waiting through the chaos as their grateful hosts prepared for the feast, she recounted the startling realization.

Months earlier as she'd awaited better waves, Marie had mentally revisited her conversation about Xea's suppressed fertility and ruminated on her continuing efforts to track the health of the group members. The jostling white water and the underlying exhilaration that surfing often brought to her shuffled the seemingly unrelated puzzle pieces together in a startlingly new way. The doctor began to speculate about the likelihood of childbearing in the near future by the three women in the group who were capable of the task. Mia had recently expressed doubts that she and Jake would produce a fifth heir, Ynez was nearly forty years old and the turmoil of pregnancy in her delicate mental state seemed ill-advised, fortunately young Xea had declared that she was not likely to be a mother for many years.

As she sat idly on the upsurging surfboard, Marie felt that she had overlooked someone.

Mixion!

The doctor quickly accessed the Master/Minion's current information about the mysterious woman who reigned over the Sovereignty in Realm 9. She was indeed quite pregnant.

Floyd contacted Bashiir later that day and they arranged a ceremonial initial visit to the Sovereignty to coincide with the birth of Mixion's child.

She and Floyd had traveled to Realm 9 yesterday and spent most of today with Bashiir in pampered comfort at a secluded bungalow on the edge of some sort of agricultural facility. Now the cordial and good-natured people of the Sovereignty were preparing a big feast in their honor. Both she and Floyd were eager to finally meet Mixion, the revered leader of the group.

As they finished their assigned tasks, each of the members of the Sovereignty stood silently behind a chair at the dinner table in the grand dining room. When a gruff old man finally shuffled to one of the three remaining seats, the secretive young woman whom Marie had seen several times during the day took her place behind the chair at the far end of the long table.

The vivacious woman spoke, "Good evening honored guests and welcome to the Sovereignty, I am Maya, Concierge and Advisor to our beloved Ruler, Mixion. Please remain comfortably seated in recognition of the esteem of which we hold you."

Maya clapped her hands twice and the others bowed obligingly.

When the young advisor had judged that the moment was right, she proclaimed, "Ladies and Gentlemen, Our Sovereign Mixion."

The ornate door to the dining room opened and a lovely and very pregnant raven-skinned woman entered with a pleasant smile.

"Good evening everyone."

Mixion tottered towards the large chair at the end of the table; Maya met the Sovereign there and helped the expectant ruler to sit. The Concierge returned to her own seat. One by one, the other members sat until the only the old man remained standing.

Mixion appraised the obsequiousness of the gentleman. "You may be seated, Landon."

The man grumbled and groaned as he plunked down.

Mixion smiled warmly to the guests, "Welcome to our world, we have been preparing with great anticipation for your arrival for many weeks. Please enjoy our hospitality."

They dined and talked for many hours.

Marie especially enjoyed the profusion of fresh fruits and vegetables that comprised much of the elaborate meal. The members of the Sovereignty took great pride in the food that they had grown on their plantation. Just as Kurt's tribe had done with animals, Mixion had 'asked' the Cotton to produce various plants that had been subsequently cultivated by the group for centuries.

With her lovely Australian accent, Mixion introduced each member of the group in turn to Floyd and Marie. The seven members were categorized by rank with Mixion undeniably in charge of the adoring group. Bashiir was positioned second and Maya third. The others were presented in descending order until only the old man remained.

"Lastly;" the Ruler tipped her head, "we have our curmudgeonly social pariah, Landon Devall."

The grumpy man refused to speak to the guests as the others had done.

Mixion smiled at the crotchety old fellow, "Landon is our Chronicler. By his own choice, he lives alone in a hut next to the Men's Compound." She carefully appraised him from across the table. "By virtue of his status as the only fertile male in the Sovereignty, through artificial insemination I assure you, he is the father of my unborn."

Landon scowled at the Monarch.

Mixion chuckled at his impropriety, "I'm afraid that Landon is also an unredeemable bigot."

• • •

Three days after the wonderful feast, Mixion went into labor. Marie set about delivering the infant with Maya's assistance in the Sovereignty's well-outfitted infirmary.

To alleviate his anxiety about the impending birth, Bashiir took Floyd on a tour of the Realm.

"We grow much of our food," the man boasted as they

walked though the many rows of vegetables at the agricultural facility. He plucked a ruby red tomato and offered it to the guest.

Floyd sampled the snack, "This is quite good. We will certainly try our hands at agronomy when we return to our Realm."

"Most of our success," Bashiir beamed, "is due to Helen's abilities and Johnny's hard work."

They watched the two middle-aged farmers as they toiled in the large field.

"Coincidentally, Helen and Maya are first cousins," Bashiir noted, "although they are vastly different people otherwise."

Floyd studied the sturdy blonde woman.

"Helen grew up on a farm near Napier on the north island of New Zealand. She is the third ranked woman in the Sovereignty. Maya spent most of her life in the bustling metropolis of Brisbane in Australia. She's the second ranked woman and nearly as sharp as Mixion."

"Has anyone ever challenged Mixion's authority?" Floyd wondered.

"No," Bashiir laughed. "Landon occasionally grumbles about having a dark-skinned leader, but no one takes him seriously."

"Marie and I were wondering how it was that Landon willingly participated in producing Mixion's baby?"

"Well he didn't," the scientist snickered. "Both of those two are repulsed by each other. Helen coaxed what was needed from him on several different occasions then Mixion took care of the rest."

Next they toured an elaborate laboratory and workshop.

"Maya and I call this the 'Technology Forge.' It really started out long ago," Bashiir admitted, "as just a crude blacksmith's shop. But over the centuries it has turned into this huge mess."

"So you and Maya work together?"

"Much of the time, yes." He sighed as he thought of the attractive young woman, "She's quite brilliant and I will dearly miss her."

"Is she going somewhere?" Floyd wondered.

The elderly man nodded, "Maya volunteered to act as the baby's nanny, which I suspect will be a full time job."

Floyd noticed an odd contraption that was partially disassembled on a nearby worktable, "What's this thing?"

"That is the prototype for our sixth generation of autonomous droids."

The engineer examined the collection of parts; "I noticed two similar robots watering the crops a few days ago from our bungalow."

"Those are the much cruder fourth generation units." Bashiir motioned to the man to follow him. Behind the laboratory was a fleet of small open vehicles, "These are our Go-Karts."

Floyd studied the diminutive cars, most seemed rather conventional, "Where are the wheels on this one?"

"That's our latest creation," Bashiir switched on the machine and it slowly rose above the ground. "We use an odd gravity defying material that is found in the floors."

The engineer nodded, "I've played around with the same stuff, my twin and I call it Gravity Amplifying Substance."

"Maya and I call it Anti-Grav."

A grayish woman peered meekly around the corner of the laboratory at the men.

Bashiir turned to the visitor, "What is it, Jen?"

"Excuse me for bothering you, sir," the dull-witted woman hesitated. "I was sent to tell you that the visiting doctor has delivered the Sovereign's baby." She paused to recall the rest of the important message, "All is well in the infirmary. I was told that the newborn will be called Lucas."

Floyd clasped Bashiir's shoulder, "Congratulations, my friend!"

• • •

On the day after the difficult birth, Mixion sat on her daybed and cradled the sleeping baby. The beaming Sovereign beckoned the guests to join her in the lavish parlor. Maya escorted the three visitors into the room.

"In thanks for the safe delivery of little Lucas," Mixion proclaimed, "and to insure the continuing spirit of friendship and cooperation between our Realms, I have directed Bashiir to assist you in your ongoing investigations of the Cerces. Any and all of our equipment and facilities are also at your disposal."

Bashiir smiled at Floyd, "Mixion told me of this partnership late last night."

"This is most generous of you and your people," Floyd thanked the Sovereign.

The new mother nodded regally. "At this time, I must admit that I have many questions about newborns for the doctor."

Marie smiled as she joined Mixion on the daybed. Apparently, she chuckled, even poised queens were prone to faltering as first time moms.

While Marie answered innumerable inquiries from Mixion and Maya about the intricacies of infant care, Floyd and Bashiir discussed the pressing needs of exploring the huge ship.

"I think that we would all benefit from some sort of quick vehicle that could travel through the Outer Causeway," Floyd told the scientist.

Bashiir rubbed his chin in thought, "I'm sure that we could modify the Anti-Grav Go-Kart to work in the passageways."

"That would be great. Anything that would reduce that long trip would really help us."

The older man considered possible improvements to the speedy little vehicle, "An airtight passenger compartment could be added to the machine."

"Ah; no more space suits in the tunnels!" Floyd cheered.

Bashiir studied the younger man, "What other endeavors shall we engage in on your behalf?"

Floyd considered the many projects that his group was currently undertaking, "My twin, whom we call Old Floyd, has traveled to the surface of the Cerces many times. Recently he discovered an immense antenna network called the 30 Gigahertz Array. Would you help him to explore the facility and hopefully reactivate it?"

"Certainly."

18. The naive sage and the savvy teen

The two very old dogs were waiting patiently together at the doorway for her, Xea listlessly noted.

"Happy thirteenth birthday!" Gunther hugged his sleepy housemate when she shuffled into the kitchen of the Castillo del Nocturno house.

The twin cats looked up blearily from the cozy bed that they shared in the corner.

Xea momentarily grimaced at the inordinately chipper man. "Thanks." She slumped onto a chair.

Gunther felt around on the countertop until he located the small sack of food. He carefully filled two bowls and placed them on the table with a large pitcher and two mugs.

She lethargically watched his morning ritual. Today Gunther seemed to have an unusual little twinkle, Xea decided.

Apparently the man could suppress his secret no longer. "I have a birthday present for you," he chirped.

Gunther produced a small bundle and handed it to her.

Xea sighed as she studied white rag that he had used to neatly package the little gift. The members of the group rarely exchanged presents, although sporadically her parents had given her little gifts during the archaic holiday of Christmas.

She had only lived with the man for a short time and he already seemed to be more thoughtful and caring than the members of her own family.

The teenager unfolded the cloth wrapping. Inside was a coppery-colored bracelet that had been crudely fashioned out of several scraps of thick wire. A curious and lopsided caricature adorned the center of the wristband. She rotated the piece in her hand for a better look and finally smiled. It was a wobbly representation of a cat's face.

Xea slipped the bracelet over her wrist, "Thank you, it's lovely."

"I'm glad that you like it," he beamed. "I worked on it for three days while you were at the clinic."

"Where did you find the wire?"

Gunther pointed downward, "There is a place at the bottom of this house were I found the thin round stuff."

"The bottom of the house?" Xea thought of the unusual way that he often described places, "The workshop in the basement?"

"Yes, the basement." His fingers found her wrist and appraisingly circumnavigated the tiny feline on the band.

Xea watched his probing digits slowly circle, "Why did you decide to make it for me?

"So you will remember me when we are apart," Gunther smiled.

Xea considered the gift. Without a doubt, no one else would have thought of presenting it to her. But she admired the significant effort that he had undertaken to secretly produce the bangle in the basement workshop. "Thank you. If I live for ten thousand years, I will always remember the gift that you gave me on my thirteenth birthday."

"Ten thousand years is a long time, right?" Gunther verified.

"Yes," Xea nodded absently. For weeks she had been teaching him about the perplexing notion of the passage of time. "It's many times longer than any born person would live."

"But clones live longer," he confirmed.

"No, they also live for about seventy or eighty years but their memories can stretch out for many thousands of years in dozens of cloned bodies."

Gunther thought about a dauntingly long period that would stretch over many millennia, "My recollections only go back to when I could see just after I came out of my mother's body."

"We guessed that was how long ago?" she asked in her most teacher-like voice.

He frowned at her question, "Nineteen or twenty years?"

"Good," she picked at the forsaken bowl of food. "You and I still only have short histories, but the clones that we know have fantastically long pasts." Xea dropped several morsels into her mouth and carefully considered the puzzling matter that she had recently investigated. "I found some strange information about the MAC clones in the Library that no one else knows."

Gunther tipped his head to listen to her secret.

"There are hidden files about all of them called dossiers. I've only studied my Aunt Marie's and it's scary."

He had a comical look of terror at her admonition, "How scary?"

"Don't tell anyone about this, Gunther. They all had many secret lives that they don't even know about."

The man nodded.

"The original version of my aunt was killed by the scanning process that recorded her memories in 2060. About a year later, she was recloned with her old memories and returned to her regular life. The scanning researchers told her that she had been in a coma during that time. Eventually she died of old age in 2113."

Xea could tell that he didn't understand much of what she had said, but it didn't matter. For over a year she had worried over the frightening implications and intricacies of the discovery.

Apparently all of the MAC clones had been secretly duplicated many different times to carry out some sort of clandestine undertaking called the CRAMP Operation. When she had tried to learn more about the nature of the enterprise all that she could find in the Library was information about minor surgical procedures to alleviate muscle spasms.

The teenager anxiously twisted the new bracelet around on her wrist, "Gunther, can you search around and find out more about this for me?"

He set his hand on Xea's, putting an end to her nervous fidgeting, "I will."

• • •

Osman sported a huge grin when he joined Floyd at the newly installed barrier door that would allow easy access to the recently refurbished Realm 18.

Floyd greeted his old friend, "It's good to see you."

The big man glanced around, "Where is everyone?"

"You're a little early."

Osman stepped through the gaping portal and fleetingly examined the tunnel that ventured off beyond. "It almost seems like we're opening up of the old west. Lots of new territory to fill up with shopping malls and mini-marts."

Floyd chuckled.

Osman rejoined Floyd by the doorway, "Tell me about your recent trip to the Sovereignty."

"It's quite a place," the engineer grinned, "I can see why they scored so high on the Hyperion Index. Every group seems to have a few unproductive members, but Mixion has admirably found appropriate duties for everyone. No one is ever idle in the Sovereignty."

"It sounds interesting, I'd love to visit there someday," Osman acknowledged.

Floyd smiled, "Funny that you should mention that, Marie and I were discussing the notion of exchanging ambassadors with the Sovereignty."

The big man considered the idea, "I would do that if the opportunity presented itself."

The two big cats ambled up to the men. Floyd reached down and stroked the back of the older feline, "Where are your people?"

The animal stared up at the engineer.

Xea shuffled slowly towards the group with Gunther plodding behind her, his outstretched hand firmly affixed to the teen's shoulder. "Here we are, Uncle Floyd."

The blind man unleashed his hand and set about carefully investigating the unfamiliar surroundings.

A noisy gaggle of four unruly schoolchildren, their beleaguered teacher and hapless parents arrived next.

Finally Marie joined the clamorous gathering.

Floyd waited solemnly for the group to quiet down. "Thank you all for coming."

Marie stood next to him at the new doorway.

"Only about fifteen years ago," the man began, "we had no idea of where we were. The notion of being only a tiny part of a giant spaceship filled with the remnants of humanity would have seemed preposterous."

He smiled at the tall woman next to him, "Then something extraordinary happened that changed everything. The Cotton produced an unknown new clone named Dr. Marie Mayfield. I clearly recall introducing her to the gang in the Rocky Mountain Camp. As we dined on a lovely lunch, Marie told us of a strange other place."

The four young students had stopped their restless squirming and listened politely to the group's nominal leader.

"A few years later we traveled to that other place, but it was a horribly devastated area filled with dead bodies and damaged robots. After we discovered the Master/Minion, I directed the robots to repair the Realm and install this door to allow easy travel."

He noticed that Marie was quite proud of her part in the epic undertaking. "Even as we stand here, far off on the opposite side of the Cerces; Old Floyd, Tin and our new friend Bashiir are preparing to explore the surface of the ship and investigate the 30 Gigahertz Array for the first time."

The crowd whispered at the mention of the exciting new adventure.

"We have recently studied uncharted areas and met many different people, but I suspect that our grand adventure has just begun." Floyd held out his arm and pointed to the opening, "Today in the spirit of our astounding progress in the last fifteen years, I dedicate the renovated Realm 18."

The group cheered.

Ynez led the students on a short tour of the new area. Mia and Jake followed along with the boisterous flock. Marie, Xea and Osman clustered around Floyd.

"Nice speech, Uncle Floyd," Xea congratulated the man.

The engineer bowed to the teenager, "Thank you."

"So what's next?" Osman asked.

Marie slipped her arm around Floyd's waist, "We're going on a grand diplomatic tour of the known regions."

"Like...what?" the big man prompted.

"Well; I've never been to Threesia," the woman said, "so we're headed there for sure. We'll also visit the Sovereignty so that I can check on Mixion and her baby." The doctor tilted her head in thought, "I'd like to make some sort of friendly gesture towards the Silkies. Perhaps we could eventually investigate their peculiar society."

Xea quivered with excitement as she listened to the details of the excursion, "Oh, please take me with you!"

Floyd frowned at the unanticipated request but Marie nodded thoughtfully to the young woman.

"Perhaps we should."

● ● ●

Later that afternoon, Xea and Gunther napped together with the two gray cats on the big bed in the tranquil attic bedroom.

On the surface of the Cerces, Bashiir jounced awkwardly about in the bulky space suit at the open airlock. Just outside, Old Floyd and Tin were tethered together to prevent accidentally launching themselves into low orbit while they labored to assemble the final parts of the Anti-Grav Go-Kart.

Bashiir handed the power unit to the engineer, "OK, that's the last piece." He clipped his safety strap to the long tether and ventured out onto the surface for the first time. "Wow! This is really amazing."

Old Floyd nodded as he affixed the power unit. In two difficult and drawn-out trips, the threesome had lugged the many modular parts from the Technology Forge in the Sovereignty to the surface airlock. The most arduous part of the journey had been squeezing the cumbersome supplies past the immobilized Minion Robot that still partially blocked the surface tunnel.

After several minor adjustments, the little vehicle was at last ready. Tin strapped himself to the improvised seat at the rear of the small vehicle, Bashiir sat in the middle and Old Floyd took the driver's seat in front. The engineer activated the antigravity system and the car stopped it's slow bobbing and gripped the surface. They sped off towards the distant dish-shaped antennas.

They stopped at the first of the massive structures. Ancient metal truss works supported the immense dish reflector. A few tiny holes perforated the circular antenna, no doubt from occasional micrometeoroids that had rained down over the millennia. After a perfunctory examination, the astronauts continued on to the next antenna.

By the time they had arrived at the eighth dish, Tin had taken to bestowing humorous names upon the otherwise identical structures.

"What are we calling this one?" the engineer asked his son.

"Ah;" the boy studied the mammoth object, "how about a hat on a stick?"

Bashiir compared the edifice to the name; "I think it looks more like sailboat made from a bathtub."

"Sailboat?" Tin wondered. "Bathtub?"

"Having never been on Earth, I don't think he knows what either of those are," Old Floyd commented.

The frivolity was interrupted by a warbling alarm. The engineer glanced at the cosmic ray detector attached to his space suit; the level of gamma radiation was swiftly rising.

Old Floyd checked the time and quickly looked around, they had nearly two hours before sunrise. Something was wrong.

"Bashiir, we're in trouble!" He swiveled around to face the scientist, "There's some sort of gamma ray shower."

"It could be from a distant supernova," the man replied. "How bad is it?"

"REALLY bad and getting worse!"

Bashiir hastily surveyed the surroundings, "We have to get under cover now!" He pointed to the left; "There's some sort of building over there."

The engineer accelerated towards the low structure. He could hear his son as he fretted about the deadly turn of events.

The warbling alarm had grown to an ear-splitting blare. The little vehicle bucked alarmingly as they approached their goal.

"I don't see anything that could shield us!" Bashiir screamed.

Old Floyd twisted the steering wheel and the Go-Kart slid around the building.

"There Dad!"

An awing projected out over a large opening some distances ahead.

In one painful jolt, the little car stopped suddenly and nearly pitched the frantic astronauts to the ground.

"We're going to have to run!" the driver screamed.

The threesome tumbled off the disabled vehicle.

The prospect of his son or the irreplaceable scientist inadvertently bouncing off into space suddenly struck the old engineer. "Hold onto each other and be careful!" he warned his companions.

The group crossed under the awning and the alarm reverted to its earlier warble. The radiation level was still too high.

Tin switched on his handheld light and shone it around under the dim overhang, "There's a door!"

Miraculously the long unused entryway opened and the refugees scrambled into the structure.

Far off in the attic bedroom, Gunther awoke with a start.

An unnerving throaty yowl filled the usually quiet attic bedroom. He felt around for his bedmate, "Xea?"

"Yeah; I hear it," she clung nervously to the blind man's hand. "Both of the cats are pacing around and making that terrible noise." There was another more sinister sound that she couldn't quite resolve.

"HELP!"

Gunther squeezed her hand in panic.

Xea gasped, it wasn't in the room. The ghostly voice was in her head.

"Help us!"

The cats leapt onto the bed and circled the frightened people.

Xea bit her lip, "It's Tin. He's never contacted me this way before. There's some sort of problem!"

Gunther slowly released his grip, "They're trapped on the surface." He was still panting, "Gamma rays? Wha...what are gamma rays?"

Xea quickly located information about the electromagnetic radiation. "It will kill them," she soberly noted.

The big animals resumed their frightful keening.

"Wait," Gunther said, "the Master/Minion says that they are inside of...Transmission Interface Facility 3."

"Xea, help me!"

"Tin! Calm down, we're trying to figure out where you are right now. Is Dad OK?" She could tell that her brother was crying.

"Yes. He and Bashiir are looking around. Dad said if we're stuck here for too long, we'll run out of air!"

"Xea;" Gunther tugged at her arm, "there's a door...and a tunnel."

"OH;" she smiled in victory, "I see it! Where does it go?"

"The passage is very long and tight but..."

She finished his sentence "...they will safely escape."

After quickly explaining the location of the passageway to Tin, Xea dashed away.

Nearly six hours later, after she had sprinted alone through the confusing maze of tunnels under the Realms, she met the exhausted astronauts just as they emerged from a narrow cableway near the Master/Minion's black chamber.

19. The grand tour

"You'll be OK," Xea tried to assure Gunther.

The blind man had a poignant look of sadness as he stood on the wide front porch of the majestic Victorian. Katoo hunkered motionlessly next to the man like a gray stone gargoyle.

Gunther kissed her cheek, "I will *really* miss you."

"I'll miss you too," Xea hoisted her bag of supplies. "Osman will check on you, Katoo and the dogs twice a day," she reminded him. The Cotton had recently reabsorbed her own big feline companion and she expected that a new version of the venerable grimalkin would eventually amble into the Cityscape.

"Don't forget," she whispered, "to work on that research into the MAC dossiers and the CRAMP Operation while I'm gone."

"I will," he nodded. "Please be careful."

"Well; I am traveling with a doctor," the teen teased him. "I don't think that there's much chance of trouble in the Sovereignty or Threesia.

Gunther frowned, "You know what I mean. You guys should stay away from the Silkies."

Xea's shoulders slumped in frustration, they had discussed this subject many times recently, "We're just going to check on them. Uncle Floyd says we'll have a robot around if anything goes wrong."

"Xea; something will happen." His hand slowly caressed her cheek, "Someone will get hurt."

• • •

"This is really impressive," Marie gawked at the towering stone castle.

Sabina smiled smugly, "Yes it is." The black robot floated diligently at her side like an ever-present tool or weapon to be unleashed when dictated by vigilance.

A wide and murky moat stretched around the robust and nearly completed walls of the mythical stone castle. Mysterious underwater creatures flitted about in the turbid liquid; their vague shimmering outlines suggested certain peril to anyone unlucky enough to plunge into the drink. The stout drawbridge of thick brown timbers slowly lowered with a protracted groan to allow the group's passage into the Palace of the Empress of Threesia.

Floyd smiled at the high drama that he had come to expect of Sabina. She had always demonstrated astonishing showmanship when presenting an imaginative new work.

Xea stood transfixed by the colossal spectacle. Marie mirthfully noted the teen's astonishment and led her safely across the bridge.

Just inside, Nick stood as the guardian of the impressive fortress adorned with chain mail armor and an immense sheathed broadsword affixed to his waist by a wide silver studded belt.

"My Empress," he bowed politely to Sabina.

She nodded curtly.

"Ladies and good sir, welcome to Threesia."

Marie stopped and studied the man with concern; the olive-colored staining of a slowly healing black eye encircled his left eye socket. She tapped on his still tender temple, "What happened here?"

He looked down with chagrin.

"He had it coming," Sabina laughed at the mortified man. "Sir Nickleby was a bit too forward with his lusty intentions towards Lady Jessica several weeks ago.

Marie tipped her head in confusion at the implied misdeed.

"She decked him when he made an imprudent pass at her."

"Really?" The doctor was flabbergasted that the skittish and high-strung woman would inflect a beating upon the charming but sometimes salacious man.

The curious group of Palace dwellers, the robotic bodyguard and the awestruck tourists wandered into the courtyard of the castle.

And there they were, Marie realized with consternation, the real life embodiment of a good portion of Kurt's Tribe.

Jessica looked up from her task of arranging food on a long plank table and Jasper stopped adjusting the placement of the many chairs for the grand banquet. Marie suddenly realized that she would know far more about their foibles and faults then they would know of hers. Sabina had undoubtedly told Jasper of his long dead twin's unending quest to hunt her down and Jessica would recall her years of dreary seclusion as a psychologically damaged mute with Marie and Ben.

Jasper waded into the entourage with an exuberant grin and an outstretched hand. "Good ta meet ya!" the big Australian squeezed Floyd with a mighty bear hug. He crouched down to Xea's eye level, "Delighted to meet you, young lady!" Finally he stood upright to consider the tall doctor, "Apparently for many years I searched about for you like an elusive phantom," he poked her shoulder to appraise her authenticity, "at last you have appeared before me more lovely than I would have ever imagined."

He was perhaps not as menacing and relentless as she had remembered.

Sabina beckoned Jessica to join them.

The young woman stood for several seconds and anxiously studied the visitors before she complied. Jessica ignored the others and crept in awe up to Marie.

She stared at the tall woman for an uncomfortably long time. Jessica finally shook her head in shame, "I could never talk to you." A thin steam of tears seeped from her eyes, "I tried but I couldn't."

"It's OK," Marie smiled and embraced the weepy woman, "We have eons ahead of us to catch up."

• • •

After several days of merriment and frivolity in Threesia, the calm steadiness of the Sovereignty was a welcome break. Before leaving Realm 3, Floyd had promised Sabina that he would acquire a speedy Go-Kart from Bashiir for her so that the Threesians could quickly traverse the Outer Causeway in the future.

During the short stay, Xea and Jessica had become good friends. Both of the young woman listened with great interest to Marie as she recounted of her horrifying nightmares of Kurt's Tribe.

Nick, Jasper and Floyd were able to rig up a colossal fire-breathing dragon that had vexed Sabina for many months. The giant mechanical monster would now greet unsuspecting visitors to the castle with an elaborate and sometimes scorching display of pyrotechnics.

Now in the dayroom of Mixion's big house, Maya held the squirmy six-month-old baby while Marie inserted the otoscope into his ear. Lucas screamed his displeasure at the procedure. Mixion looked on with concern.

"Everything seems fine," the doctor smiled at the pouty young patient.

Xea offered the boy a favorite toy and he cooed at the distraction.

"Maya;" the Sovereign directed, "will you feed Lucas and Xea some lunch please."

The devoted assistant bowed slightly and ventured off to the dining room with her two charges.

Mixion watched Marie pack the medical instruments back into her red satchel.

"I understand that you and Floyd can command the Cotton to produce clones with a variety of qualities now," the woman said.

"Within reason, yes. Why are you interested?"

Mixion appraised the doctor for several seconds before answering, "I hope to produce another heir," she stroked her chin in thought, "but I'd prefer a more tolerant and willing sperm donor."

The queen was carefully choosing her suitors, Marie realized. "What do you have in mind, Mixion?"

"Landon is quite old and much too prickly to father my children and carry on his important work as the Chronicler of the Sovereignty."

"Without a doubt," Marie agreed.

"Ultimately, I'd favor combining my genetic line with Maya's. Our offspring would be splendidly suited for leadership, social organization and technical achievements."

The doctor nodded. "Eventually I think that would be a

possible way to produce super kids, but for now we are stuck with the limitations of the available stock."

"Yes, I had surmised that. If you find it acceptable, Marie, I would greatly appreciate a fertile young clone of Bashiir to father my future children."

"I will see what I can do." The doctor tilted her head towards the Sovereign, "But I have a request of you as a fair exchange."

"I will entertain any reasonable demands," the shrewd ruler answered.

"Floyd and I would like have our dear friend Osman live amongst you as our representative."

"An ambassador," Mixion acknowledged, "that would be an excellent idea."

20. Diplomacy

They stopped in the dim tunnel.

"According to Gunther, this is the edge of the Silkie encampment," Xea told Floyd. "That aperture door over there leads to the Ritual Pool."

The man glanced back at Marie who waited some distance back in the passageway. The doctor waved as she stood next to the Minion Robot bodyguard that they had summoned for the problematical meeting.

The threesome had agreed earlier that Xea and Floyd would make the initial contact with the volatile cult while Marie stayed behind for now with the robot. If the group seemed placid and approachable, the doctor would join them.

• • •

Gunther sat on the edge of the bed. The steady ticking of the desk clock was the only sound in the lonely habitat. He slid his hand slowly over the rumpled blankets until he located the dozing cat. The animal's head bobbed up when the man awoke it. Katoo voiced an odd chirp before it leapt to the floor, determined to find a more restful place to sleep.

"They're with the Silkies," Gunther reported to his feline companion, although he was quite certain that the big animal was well aware of the meeting.

He stood and felt his way across the room to the side table. Gunther's fingers found the stalwart windup clock. Xea had pried the clock glass away from the timepiece weeks ago when she taught him how to use the device. The blind man carefully appraised the positions of the two metal hands, it was 3:12 in the morning, he decided. Seven minutes later than the last time that he had checked.

Gunther tottered back to the bed and sat glumly. For most of the night he had fretted about the devilry that the Silkies might inflict upon his cherished friends.

• • •

Xea peered tentatively through the slit of the aperture door. Several members of the Cult were engaged in some sort of food preparation. A robed young man conversed in hushed tones with a similarly attired elderly man; no doubt the old priest and his assistant, Xea realized.

She withdrew from the surreptitious view port.

"Nothing much is going on," the teen whispered to Floyd.

"OK," he replied, "let's go with the original plan." The man smiled at his nervous niece, "Try to project confidence, and don't worry, I'll be watching over you the whole time."

Xea nodded anxiously. She stepped through the opening and waited for someone to notice her arrival.

The acolyte pointed at the intruder and the priest spun around to glare at the teen. The old man's frightening look of hatred dissolved at the sight of the docile and diminutive visitor. The younger man had drawn a crude but formidable knife from his robe but the Holy man waved him off.

The two men approached Xea. As Gunther had suggested,

she bowed to the cleric. "We have come to seek your wisdom," Xea intoned in a trembling whisper.

"Face me," the priest demanded.

She complied.

The Holy man pointed to the visitor and the acolyte carefully frisked the teen for concealed weapons. Xea quietly endured the protracted probing by the young man.

When he was satisfied that the intruder posed no threat, the old man at last smiled, "Welcome to you, my young pilgrim. From where have you come?"

Xea recited the vague and carefully worded reply that was essentially true and likely to be accepted favorably by the vain cleric, "I have come from far away with my kin to seek out further enlightenment."

The old man relished the implied importance of the declaration, "You are free to partake of our wisdom." He held out his hand to stop her, "But first, tell me of the kin who has accompanied you here."

"My uncle," she stammered, "my uncle also wishes to meet your holiness."

The acolyte again drew his knife.

The High Priest frowned, "Where is this man?"

Xea turned towards the aperture door. The elastic white flap fluttered and Floyd stepped through to join the teenager. He too was subjected to a complete search for contraband.

The old man finally motioned for the travelers to follow, "Partake of our morning prayers."

• • •

"Xea, can you hear me?" Gunther called out to his soul mate.

"Yes. Uncle Floyd and I are in the Sanctum. The Silkies are in the middle of their morning prayer ritual right now."

The blind man sighed with relief, *"Where is your aunt?"*

"She's still waiting in the tunnel with a Minion Robot."

"Don't let her wait too long," Gunther warned, *"the grumpy old coot will think that you are planning an attack if he finds her hiding outside."*

"OK. I'll get her when the ritual is complete."

The big cat nuzzled his arm as he laid upon the bed, *"Be careful, Xea."*

"I will."

• • •

"I know you," the priest said flatly to Marie.

"Yes," she replied matter-of-factly to the old man as the assistant searched her for weapons. "I led the blind man away a few years ago."

"What became of the devil child?" the cleric smirked.

Marie stared defiantly at the priest, "He's in a better place now."

The acolyte finished his gruff inspection.

The Holy man tipped his head in query, "I trust that the machine enforcers will not disturb our friendly gathering?"

The woman shrugged, "If it remains truly friendly."

"Then come and join the faithful in celebration," he beckoned.

• • •

The acolyte pointed to the low round pedestal in the center of the shrine, "You will kneel there in front of the altar."

Floyd nodded respectfully to the terse assistant and motioned for Xea and Marie to proceed.

"No!" the man snapped. "Only the adults in front." He gestured to an empty spot on the floor between two of the faithful, "The juvenile must stay there."

Xea stared uneasily at her uncle.

He motioned to the spot and smiled tepidly.

The teen ventured back and knelt with the others. She watched the acolyte lead the adults to the altar and stand quietly behind them as they knelt.

"Gunther, can you hear me?"

"What's happening now, my friend?"

Xea furtively glanced around the dim chamber, *"We're kneeling in the shrine with the Silkies. I think we're waiting for something."*

"Probably for the old priest," Gunther guessed.

Just as the blind man had suggested, the elderly cleric hobbled to the altar and faced the followers.

"We are brought here today," he boomed, "to extol the almighty Spirit of the Sacred Silk." The old man brought his palms together, "Let us pray."

Xea imitated the surrounding zealots and stared at the floor.

After nearly a minute of silent reflection, the priest continued, "We have pilgrims amongst us today, visitors from an unenlightened land who seek out our sole repository of the truth." The cleric grinned scornfully at the kneeling outsiders. "In commemoration of this blessed event, we will undertake the very rare cleansing ritual to rid the evil from our presence."

The Holy man produced a small brown bowl with an intricately decorated cover from a fold in his robe. He lifted the lid and a cloud of bluish gray smoke swirled angrily from the vessel. The acrid plume quickly spread over the visitors.

Xea's eyes watered from the overwhelming haze. Her vision suddenly fractured into madly oscillating flashes of color.

Something was wrong!

"Gunther! Help!"

In strangely flickering still pictures, she could see the priest slowly raise his arms above his head.

"Wha...what's happening Xea?"

The cleric's fingers interlocked as if he was clutching something.

"Gunther, I can't move. Everything is spinning!"

"The old man! XEA!"

The teen felt the arms of the followers wrap around her like constricting ropes.

"Xea! What's the priest doing?"

She struggled against the strangling constraints. *"He's...he's moving his arms up and down."* She was going to vomit, *"Like he's pounding...something."*

"It's a signal!" The blind man suddenly recalled a gruesome past ritual, *"QUICK! What about the acolyte?"*

"He's holding the...OH NO! He's going to stab Aunt Marie!" Xea flinched as the zealots wrestled her down. She must contact the Master/Minion!

As the frenzied followers of the wicked old man pummeled the helpless teen, she implored the cyber overseer to intercede, but to no avail.

• • •

"NO!" Gunther screamed.

He had just seconds to save them.

The blind man clenched his head in agony as he thrashed about on the bed.

"AHHH!"

IT WAS ALREADY TOO LATE FOR ONE OF THEM!

Where were the Minions? Tears ran down his face.

"Quick! QUICK!" he begged as he marshaled his distant allies.

Good, now another! AHHH!

Gunther jerked; he could feel the torturous injuries as they were inflicted on his companions.

"NO!"

Finally in exhaustion, his hands slid limply from his head.

The robots were successful, he suddenly realized. Two had been saved.

Gunther panted from the horrific ordeal.

The clock ticked indifferently in the peaceful little bedroom.

The blind man balled his fists tightly in growing rage at the Silkies' sneak attack.

In spiteful vengeance he willing allowed the proposed retribution.

• • •

The smoke was dissipating.

A Minion Robot forced the pallid and twitching carcass into the gray mound. With a spare mechanical appendage, it pried his fingers from hers and nudged the quivering man away.

Floyd stared in horror as Marie's bloody and nearly lifeless body was consumed by the writhing silver fibers.

His cherished mate of sixteen years was gone.

The excruciating yelps of the Silkies filled the Holy Sanctum of the Silk as the methodical robot executioners felled the last of the zealots. The seven members of the cult lay dead or dying around the altar.

Xea pushed her way past the gore and pressed her bruised and tearstained face against his shoulder. "I tried to call the Minion Robots to protect you but my pleas were denied!" she wailed.

Floyd winced at the young woman's revelation. Marie might still be alive, he realized, had he thought to lift Xea's long prohibition against commanding the machines.

The threads constricted into a tight bundle. The Minion that had delivered the woman's body drifted away from the mournful humans.

Floyd brushed the splattered blood from his cheek in shocked detachment; there dangling above the mound of slowly contorting Cotton was the precious pocket watch that Marie had lost to the old priest nearly two years before.

21. A torrent of attainment

"It's time," Mia looked up at the vibrating cocoon.

Floyd adjusted his position on the low bench. He'd been waiting with her for hours.

A ghastly muffled scream emanated from one end of the gray capsule.

Mia nodded, "I told you."

She was right, Floyd realized. Her many thousands of years of experience with the production of clones had led her to predict that it would happen.

The piercing cry subsided and the esteemed tender of the Cotton set to work.

As the hours slowly drifted by, he quietly watched Mia work from his spot on the bench.

Four days after hearing of Marie's murder and reabsorption by the Cotton in the Silkie Realm, Mia had noticed that a new cocoon was developing in the long quiescent gray mound of her own Realm. The occupant of the capsule remained unknown until Floyd and Xea returned to confirm with great relief that a new Marie clone was slowly being assembled by the odd fibrous life form.

Xea had since discovered the Master/Minion's unequivocal protocol for the rapidly recloning of the human masters of the Cerces in the event of disaster.

It was eerily like the last time that it she'd appeared more than sixteen years before, Floyd thought, but now instead of a mysterious newcomer, they knew exactly what to expect of the soon to be released clone.

He stood to get a better view of the proceedings.

Mia gently removed a large piece of silvery matting and there she was again.

Marie's eyes fluttered and slowly opened.

Floyd slid his fingers lightly over his long-lost mate's cheeks and she smiled.

"Welcome back, my love," he whispered.

• • •

Hours later, tattered bits of the cocoon laid everywhere. Marie rested limply on the bench clad in baggy blue overalls.

"Let's go home," the man beckoned.

"I can't," the doctor sighed, "I'm too tired to plod all of the way back to the Beach Habitat right now."

Mia and Floyd giggled at the inside joke.

With a silly little fanfare, Floyd bowed to the slumped woman, "Not to worry, my lady. A carriage awaits to carry you off to the manor house."

Marie was perplexed by the strange show.

Mia and Floyd helped the weary woman to the tunnel. On either side of the aperture door in the long dark passageway were parked two of Bashiir's sleek Go-Karts.

The bleary doctor studied the vehicles for a moment, "This is new."

"There's been quite a few changes in the last eight months," Floyd mused.

After several minutes of fumbling about with the low-slung machine, they sped off for the Beach Habitat.

Ten minutes later, the engineer parked the jaunty little car at their destination and assisted Marie through the Polynesian jungle to the beach hut. The languid woman studied the roiling gray breakers for several minutes before trudging to the soft mat. Within minutes of lying down, the doctor slept.

When Marie awoke, their cozy home was filled with the ruby glow of a spectacular sunset. Floyd had joined her on the sleeping mat and was softly snoring. She caressed his shoulders and he stirred.

They shared a passionate kiss. The man studied the rejuvenated young woman for many minutes in the gradually waning light.

"I wasn't really aware of how much you meant to me," Floyd wiped his damp eyes, "until you were gone."

"After your murder, I was a mess," he recounted. "If it hadn't been for Xea's resourcefulness, I'd still be curled up in a ball on the floor of the Sanctum."

224

"What happened?" Marie wondered.

"Even with a broken arm and several cracked ribs, she managed to contact Threesia and the Sovereignty. Within a few hours, Sabina and Nick arrived to treat us. Bashiir appeared the next day with a hastily modified Go-Kart. They hauled us back to the infirmary in the Sovereignty where Maya and Mixion patched us up."

She considered the tale for a time, "How did Xea's arm fair?"

"It seems to be fine, although it's not very straight."

The doctor nodded, "It's really difficult to set broken bones correctly without X-rays. What happened here during our unfortunate altercation?"

"That was remarkable too, Gunther summoned the robots that saved Xea and me. When it was all over, he contacted both Mia and Tin. They eventually found him sobbing in the basement workshop. Tin stayed with him in the Cityscape for several days until we returned."

"Poor guy," Marie said.

"It was really touching when we returned, he and Xea vowed to never part again. Now they're inseparable," he smiled.

"Mmm;" Marie winked, "in love, I suspect."

"So it seems."

"It's really cute, if you think about it," she smoothed the

splayed strands of gray hair above his ears, "they each have rescued the other."

• • •

"Alright;" Marie said as they lounged together on a big blanket laid upon the warm black sand beach, "catch me up on what's happened in the last eight months."

"Your murder quickly led to the most important change," Floyd remarked, "a strong new alliance of our group with the Threesians and the Sovereignty quickly developed to carefully monitor and eventually assimilate the others onboard the Cerces."

She listened closely as he recounted the events.

"Mixion and Jasper are concocting a set of protocols for interacting for the first time with the residents of the remaining fifteen Realms."

Marie nodded, "Any preliminary suggestions?"

"Yes;" Floyd laughed, "they both decided that we should use Minion Robots as spies."

"That's a good idea, since presumably all of the Realms have the machines floating about already, no one would notice anything out of the ordinary."

"Let's see, what else?" Floyd thought. "Sabina, Jasper, Nick and Jessica have been working away in Threesia. According to Sabina, the main part of the castle is nearly complete. The big news in Realm 3 is that they have a new cocoon developing in the Cotton."

"Who?"

"Gunther suggested that his mother could be added to the group and Sabina eventually agreed. Now we're all waiting for a Leona 1 clone to hatch."

"Two things occur to me," Marie frowned. "So we haven't given up hope on the Silkies?"

"No. Mixion and I think that the followers were probably just ordinary people who were brainwashed and manipulated by the old priest."

"If Leona is Gunther's mom, why is the Master/Minion duplicating her? Doesn't that violate the rule against cloning parents?" Marie wondered.

Floyd shrugged, "I guess it does, but I just instructed the cyber overlord to do it and the Master/Minion carried out the task."

Marie considered the inconsistency for several seconds, "I'll have to look into that later. How's Osman?"

"He and Bashiir have swapped Realms. Osman is our ambassador to the Sovereignty and Bashiir represents Mixion's interests here."

"How are the two diplomats doing?" she chuckled.

"They're both here right now for an important official meeting. I'm told that Mixion is smitten with Osman and is considering him as a future father for her heirs."

Marie laughed, "Everybody *loves* Osman."

"Bashiir has been working nonstop with Old Floyd and Tin. They managed to get the 30 Gigahertz Array working although still not very well."

"Have they found anything new?" she wondered.

"Nothing intelligible from Earth but we realized recently that a 30 Gigahertz signal is greatly attenuated by the atmosphere, so there's still hope. Bashiir discovered a sister ship called the Cerces 2 which is trailing us in orbit."

"Have they talked to anyone there?"

"No," he said sadly. "They've interacted with the Master/ Minion on the Cerces 2, but apparently the vessel was damaged long ago and the M/M doesn't seem to know what's become of the Human Test Subjects onboard."

Marie sighed, "I guess we should eventually explore the Cerces 2."

"We're way ahead of you," the engineer chortled. "Gunther and Xea think that we could produce several Kat clones over there if we can find some viable Cotton on the ship."

"Oh! That's a great idea. We wouldn't have to risk any people with the long trip and the uncertain conditions at the destination." Marie mentally tallied up all of her good friends, "What about Ynez?"

"You'll be especially proud of your young medical protégé," Floyd noted. "Xea spent several days investigating Ynez's sorry mental state and she concocted a remedy involving some hormonal adjustments, more induced euphoria and something that reminds me of

Transcendental Meditation."

"And?" Marie prompted.

"It seems to have worked, Ynez has snapped out of her odd funk."

"Well;" Marie teased her mate, "while I've been slouching around for months on vacation, you guys have actually accomplished something!"

• • •

"Hi!" Marie hugged Mixion. Lucas cooed happily at the doctor as the Sovereign held the chubby toddler.

After several days of marvelous rest with Floyd in the Hawaiian Beach Habitat, they had ventured to the Cityscape for the Street Fair. Sabina and Xea had organized the impromptu celebration for the chance gathering of so many people in Realm 17.

Bashiir and Osman joined the royal entourage. Both men stared at the recently returned doctor while she played with the little boy.

Marie laughed at the gawking twosome; "I feel strangely like a celebrity now."

"No one can quite believe that you've returned from the dead apparently unscathed," Osman noted.

"Yes," the woman mused. "Just a few minutes ago, Gunther thoroughly checked me over to assure himself that I was real."

Distant music wafted through the air.

"Is that a guitar that I hear?" Marie wondered.

Osman nodded, "Isn't it great! Ynez has taken up playing the old instrument again after so many years." He winked at the doctor, "Old Floyd says that she's finally feeling much better about life."

Perhaps Xea's biochemical tinkering had worked with Ynez when nothing else had, Marie speculated.

"Visitors to the Cityscape!" Sabina shouted as she stood on the bench in the center of park-like common backyard. "Please gather around."

The milling throng of residents and guests slowly assembled around the old artist.

"It's so nice to be here again," Sabina noted, "and for the first time with so many new faces." She pointed at Floyd, "With the full consent of the all powerful leader of this now substandard region of the Cerces, I'd like to make a few announcements."

The mob laughed at the friendly inter-Realm jab.

"This little soiree," Sabina continued, "is in honor of the visiting dignitaries from the far-flung Sovereignty and another more fanciful Kingdom of which I am personally associated with, the fantastic land of Threesia."

An enthusiastic cheer echoed between the tall houses that encircled the huge backyard.

The flamboyant woman held out her arms, "Wait, there's more. Mia, the local chronicler, tells me that the big event is actually in three days, but we certainly can recognize it now. Xea will soon be fourteen years old!"

Old Floyd and Ynez smiled proudly at their now nearly grown first-born.

"Once again with the full approval of the various luminaries amongst us, I have been authorized to bestow upon Xea the grand title of Supreme Librarian of All Human Knowledge."

No one clamored louder than Gunther at the proclamation as he stood next his beaming dark haired housemate.

When the stupendous applause finally subsided, Sabina continued, "As the result of a tragic murder many months ago, the assorted provincial Realms of the Cerces 4 came together to form a strong alliance to further the well being of our tiny remnant of humanity." She smiled warmly at the doctor, "We'd like to all welcome back our highly regarded physician, ever-intrepid adventurer and exceptional administrator of the ship; Marie 3.1."

The doctor blushed at the extravagant attention before she bowed to the cheering crowd, "Thank you all!"

"Food will be served shortly!" Sabina announced before she jumped from the bench and joined the swarm that was developing around Marie.

Xea and Gunther pushed through the crowd.

"Hi Aunt Marie!" the diminutive teen said.

For a brief instant, the doctor studied young Xea as she stood next to the now decidedly middle-aged Sabina. Just as she had predicted long ago during a checkup, the teen was nearly as tall as the venerable artist.

Marie tussled the teenager's hair, "Thanks to you and Gunther for all of the great work that you've done while I was away. How's your arm?"

Xea stretched out her slightly bent appendage for her aunt to inspect.

Marie shrugged, "Good enough, I suppose."

The merry carnival-like atmosphere of the Street Fair was infectious.

"OK everybody," Xea announced to the dozen or so bystanders, "Gunther and I have this great new trick that we'd like to share with you."

The blind man could not contain himself, "We figured this out a few days ago when Tin was visiting and now we want to try it out on you."

"Hopefully it's not too painful," Sabina joked.

Xea whispered instructions to Gunther and he nodded. The blind man idly stroked his chin in thought for several seconds.

"We need a little space here," Xea directed everyone to form a large circle. She then set about staring intently at each of the audience members in turn. When at last she was done, Xea squeezed Gunther's hand.

The audience pitched back in surprise.

An immense fire-breathing dragon inexplicably appeared before them, lumbering menacingly from side to side as orange flames sporadically erupted from the beast's huge mouth.

Sabina and Jessica were the first to recognize the clever ruse.

"That's the fierce guardian at the Threesia castle moat," Sabina declared.

"How did you do that?" Floyd asked.

Xea blinked several times and the illusion faded, "We discovered how to create a group hallucination. Gunther directed Sebastian to wake up the dragon and I pushed the image of the encounter from the robot's cameras into each of your brains at the same time."

"That was *really* scary," Marie acknowledged. "Can you do it again?"

The two talented illusionists nodded in unison.

"This comes from one of the cameras on the surface of the Cerces," Xea told the group. "Gunther has pondered this image for hours." She gazed at each of the spectators.

A giant slowly rotating sphere appeared. The mottled blue surface of the world was strewn with a few brown and green patches. Fluffy white masses billowed gracefully across the surface of the planet.

Most of the audience sighed at the elegant floating spectacle.

It was the Earth.

The group pined nostalgically for their long forsaken home world.

Sabina finally voiced what they were all thinking, "We have to go back...."

Appendix

<u>The clone numbering scheme</u>
The number "5" in Floyd 5.136 is the version number of the clone. There can be hundreds or even thousands of a particular version of a clone; each starts out as a twenty-five-year-old with identical memories. Most copies of any version live ordinary lives of fifty or sixty years before dying of natural causes or unfortunate accidents. Rarely a clone is "called back" and reabsorbed by the Cotton. When the clone next appears sometime later, the version number will be advanced by one.

The number "136" in Floyd 5.136 is the sequence number. Floyd 5.136 is the 136th copy of the 5th version that the Cotton had initiated. The clones noticed early on that the Cotton often skipped several numbers: Floyd 5.127+ was followed by Floyd 5.136, skipping eleven numbers. Mia had noticed, much to her dismay, that the Cotton occasionally produced a cocoon only to reabsorb it sometime later without yielding a new clone. Although this idea seemed to account for some of the "missing" sequence numbers, it was still an unsatisfying explanation. Floyd guessed much later that the Cotton might have discontinued some clonings at a very early stage for various reasons.

The "plus sign" in Floyd 5.127+, Ynez 3.79+, Nick 4.1+, Mia 11.1+ and Jake 2.2+ denotes that these copies are capable of sexual reproduction. Floyd 5.127+ and Ynez 3.79+ were produced to evaluate the group's ability to reproduce sexually without artificial means and to successfully raise and care for the offspring. Nick 3.551, Mia 10.8 and Jake 1.572 chose to be sexually reproductive after the discovery of the Master/Minion, apparently forgoing any future clonings for the privilege.

The Hyperion Index of Societal Evolution

Extracted from the memoirs of Juno Marquesas

The Hyperion Index is an extensive set of measurements developed by Professor Juno Marquesas in 2788 that allowed for the first time accurate mathematical calculations for modeling a society's evolution. Professor Marquesas, who was widely regarded as the "Charles Darwin" of Societal Evolution received a Nobel Prize for his work on the Hyperion Index in 2794.

The major elements of the Hyperion Index:

A society must evolve on its own from a "Stone Age" to "Industrial Revolution" level without outside assistance.

A society must care for all of its members including the ill, elderly, misfit and dissident.

A society must show a strong desire to advance their lot, typically by exploration and experimentation.

A society must be accepting of outsiders.

A society must not actively or passively destroy their environment or damage it in such a way as to lead to its destruction.

A society must be capable of reproducing without artificial means and must successfully raise and care for their offspring.

A society must allow for the self-determination of its members.

A successful society must accept unpopular ideas when faced with strong validating evidence.

Selected Hyperion Index comparisons of Human Test Groups aboard the Cerces 4 before the discovery of the Master/Minion Scores assigned by the Master/Minion are listed in gray.

Index Point	Floyd's Group	Kurt's Tribe	The Silkies	Sovereignty
1) Self evolution from Stone Age to Industrial Revolution	Yes 69	partial 52	No 27	Yes 78
2) Care of weak members	Yes-Nick, Jake 75	No-Boy & Girl X 18	No- Gunther 41	Yes- Landon 71
3) Strong desire to advance their society though the development of culture and technology	Yes- exploration & experimentation 83	Partial- by the development of weapons & explosives 33	No- little desire to advance 12	Yes - tools, agriculture, advanced technology 88
4) Acceptance of outsiders	Yes- Mostly accepted Marie wholeheartedly 81	Partial- Exile of Marie 1, acceptance of Marie 2 29	Partial- initial acceptance 36	Yes- Easily accepted Bashiir 2 89
5) Activities leading to environment damage	Minor damage 75	Greatly damaged in Robot War 9	Moderate damage 45	Minor damage 81
6) Capable of sexual reproduction & successful care of offspring	Yes- Xea 92	Unknown 50	Partial- lack of care for Gunther 62	Yes- Mixion has been pregnant.No baby was delivered 75
7) Allows self-determination by individuals	Yes- pseudo shared leadership 84	Poor- megalomaniac leader 21	Poor to moderate 42	Yes - Strong, fair leadership model 73
8) Acceptance of unpopular ideas when faced with strong validating evidence	Highly accepting 88	Not accepting 9	Not accepting 8	Extremely accepting 91
9) Details have been restricted by the Master/Minion				
10) Details have been restricted by the Master/Minion				
Rating by M/M 0 = unevolved 1000 = Most highly evolved	712	253	334	754

The scoring:

2) Weak members are nonproductive, elderly, immature, disabled, mentally unstable, ill, misfit or dissident members of a group.

5) Environmental damage:

Initial extreme damage that leads to immediate extinction = 0
Later extreme damage that leads to extinction = 7
Extreme damage that does not lead to extinction = 18
Severe damage = 26
Moderate damage = 36
"Typically expected damage" or median value = 52
Fair damage = 67
Minor damage = 78
Insignificant damage = 90
No damage = 100

6) Capable of Sexual reproduction and the subsequent quality of care for the offspring

Because most societies after 2050 have been composed of a mix of clones and sexually produced non-clones, this index number is determined in two parts.

Part 1:
Not capable or capable but never undertaken = 0
Unknown or undetermined capabilities = 25
Capable of sexual reproduction = 50

Part 2:
This number can span from 0 to 50. Below is a guide.
No members cared for offspring resulting in immediate death = 0
Insignificant care resulting in swift death = 3
Insignificant care leading to early childhood death = 6
Insignificant care leading to death before adulthood = 9
Insignificant care not leading to death = 12
Moderate care by a small fraction of group (usually a parent) = 16
Moderate care by a large portion of group = 19
Moderate care by most of group = 22
Unknown,unattemped or undetermined capabilities = 25
Moderate care by entire group = 25
Significant care by a small fraction of group (usually a parent) = 28
Significant care by a large portion of group = 31
Significant care by most of group = 34
Significant care by entire group = 37
Exemplarily care by a small fraction of group (usually a parent) = 41
Exemplarily care by a large portion of group = 44
Exemplarily care by most of group = 47
Exemplarily care by entire group = 50

7) Allows self determination by group members: This number varies between 0 and 50. A group that rigidly predetermines all individuals positions for all of its history will score very low. Groups with strong individual leaders that dictate individual group members positions will score somewhat higher. Shared leadership and strong "Fair" leadership will score still higher. A group that allows complete self determination by all individuals at all times during its entire history will score very high.

I recall waking up very early on the morning of July 30th 2010.

It was warm and very dark. I quickly realized that I wasn't in my familiar old bed in my ancient Ranch-style house in California. As I have often written in many different novels, it was one of those rare times when the waking mind takes a few minutes to fully comprehend exactly what is going on.

In retrospect that particular conundrum is often quite amusing. In *Xea in the Library of All Human Knowledge* Marie labors through this very problem at the beginning of Chapter 2. I wrote about her early morning bewilderment shortly after my own on the morning of July 30th.

As I lay in an unusually plush bed, I could hear waves breaking on a shore very nearby. This, I realized, does not happen in the inland valleys of Northern California.

Where was I?

Oddly, I could also just barely make out faint mewing.

I got up to peer through a wide sliding glass patio door hidden behind a set of dark brown curtains.

It seemed that I had been sleeping in a little cottage overlooking a small stretch of grass bestrewn with several tall coconut palms. Just beyond was the pale blue of the restless Pacific Ocean.

The mental puzzle pieces came together: I was with my wife on the north shore of Oahu for our wedding anniversary.

But what of the mewing? Did I dream of a cat? I had certainly been missing my beloved gray Tabby, but he was at home with my son in California.

As I gazed out at the endless Hawaiian breakers, a tiny black kitten dashed up to the patio door.

He looked up expectantly and mewed. I slide the door open and the little scamp scrambled into our cottage. We played with him for quite a while. Friendly little ferals, it turns out, are common around hotels in Hawaii. We discovered during late night walks around the resort that a dozen or so felines of various ages would clean up the Room Service trays that guests left at the front doors of the cottages for the wait staff to retrieve.

We jokingly named *our* little cottage cat the "Mahalo Kitten."

Mahalo is a general expression of gratitude in the Hawaiian language. Translated into English, it has come to mean "Thank you."

The Mahalo Kitten visited us often during the four days that we spent in the Hawaiian cottage that overlooked the Pacific Ocean. I took to writing the chapter summaries for *Xea in the Library of All Human Knowledge* at a small round wooden table just outside of the back door.

More than once, a friendly black kitten sat purring in my lap as I worked. I like to think that the little feline deserves some of the credit for the book.

Mahalo, Kitten.

Regards,

SF Chapman
Northern California, USA
September 2015

Science Fiction Adventure

They were ordinary people: An artist, an engineer, a secretary, a carpenter, a teacher, a restaurateur and a surfer. They had very little in common and likely would never have come upon each other were it not for the novelty of their propagation.

Late in 2034, all were conceived as some of the very few Mildly Altered Clones that would ever be produced.

By chance, a Genetics Researcher had come upon the names and particulars of these Mildly Altered Clones and sought them out for an astonishing new project.

Many thousands of years later the engineer, the secretary, the artist, the surfer, the teacher, the restaurateur and the carpenter finally met.

Amongst the first few questions that they asked of each other was this: "Where are we?"

Available in paperback everywhere and as a Kindle eBook at Amazon.com

If you enjoyed *Xea in the Library of All Human Knowledge* by S F Chapman, you might also like *The Ripple in Space Time*

THE RIPPLE IN SPACE-TIME
FREE CITY BOOK 1
S F CHAPMAN

<u>Science Fiction Detective Adventure</u>

Inspector Ryo Trop of the Free City Inquisitor's Office is called in when the Lunar Ultra Energy Lab is destroyed by a mysterious blast. Ryo quickly discovers that a complex and sinister scheme is afoot as he searches for clues in the moldering feudal fiefdoms of the Warlords that dominate human affairs in 2445.

As he struggles with the difficult case, the same question keeps popping up: Could the recent wave of space piracy be connected to the disaster?

Available in paperback everywhere and as a Kindle eBook at Amazon.com

You might also enjoy *Torn From On High* by S F Chapman

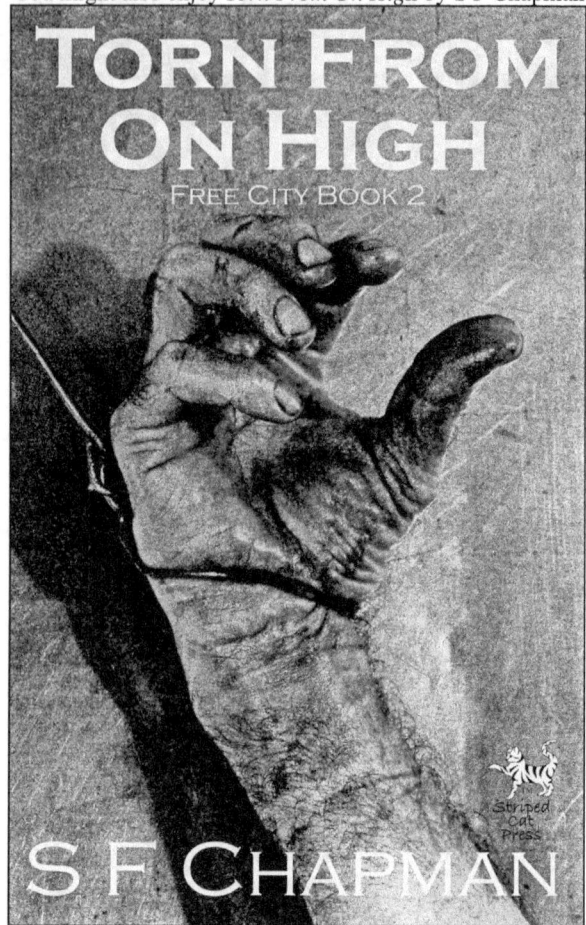

<u>Science Fiction Detective Adventure</u>

Called out of early retirement, Inspector Trop and his longtime friend Spy Master Lieutenant Zmuda discover a clandestine plot for human domination in the Sahara Desert and a nefarious effort to kill Space Debris Salvage workers in Low Earth Orbit.

As both men struggle with their difficult investigations, they learn that the cases are linked through a tangled web of duplicity and murder.

Available in paperback everywhere and as a Kindle eBook at Amazon.com

After retiring from the construction industry, S F Chapman set about writing 8 novels in 5 short years.

His first, *Floyd 5.136 -- The MAC Series Book 1*, is a tale of human clones from the mid 21st century unwittingly trapped in a strange world in the far future. His second is a drama entitled *On the Back of the Beast* about an earthquake that destroys Northern California.

Mr. Chapman has completed two sequels to *Floyd 5.136* called *Xea in the Library of All Human Knowledge* and *Beyond the Habitable Limit*. He is currently working on the fourth book in The MAC Series. Other Science Fiction pieces include *The Ripple in Space-Time* and *Torn From On High*.

The author has also produced two literary fiction novels: *I'm here to help* about a series of minor errors that lead to the unintended adoption of a newborn girl and a gritty novel about homelessness called *The Missive in the Margins*.

www.ingramcontent.com/pod-product-compliance
Lightning Source LLC
Chambersburg PA
CBHW060541260626
47161CB00003B/999